THE
AMAZING
ADVENTURES OF

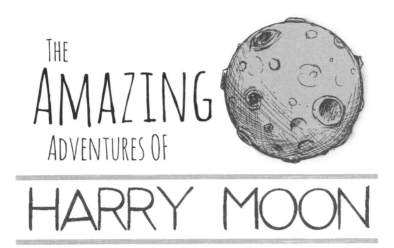

HARRY MOON

THE SCARY SMART HOUSE

by
Mark Andrew Poe

Illustrations by Christina Weidman

rabbit  publishers

The Scary Smart House (The Amazing Adventures of Harry Moon,
by Mark Andrew Poe

Rabbit Publishers
1624 W. Northwest Highway
Arlington Heights, IL 60004

Illustrations by Christina Weidman
Cover Design by Chris D'Antonio
Interior Design by Lewis Design & Marketing
Creative Consultants: David Kirkpatrick, Thom Black and Paul Lewis

ISBN: 978-1-943785-30-8

10 9 8 7 6 5 4 3 2 1

1. Fiction - Action and Adventure 2. Children's Fiction
First Edition
Printed in U.S.A.

"Let's just say I have
been around this block
a lot longer than Siri"

~ *RABBIT*

TABLE OF CONTENTS

H

PREFACE

Halloween visited the little town of Sleepy Hollow and never left.

Many moons ago, a sly and evil mayor found the powers of darkness helpful in building Sleepy Hollow into "Spooky Town," one of the country's most celebrated attractions. Now, years later, a young eighth grade magician, Harry Moon, is chosen by the powers of light to do battle against the mayor and his evil consorts.

Welcome to *The Amazing Adventures of Harry Moon*. Darkness may have found a home in Sleepy Hollow, but if young Harry has anything to say about it, darkness will not be staying.

THE KNIGHTINGALE KNIGHTS

"Harry, you'll need to hurry." Harry's mom handed him a large, manilla envelope. "It has to be postmarked by five."

"Don't worry," Harry said. "I'll make it. But she's really pushing the limit."

"I know," Mom said as Harry stuffed the envelope into his backpack. "The flu slowed her down."

"No problem, Mom," Harry said. He was pumped. *Duty.* Harry Moon had a duty to his family. He looked at the grandfather clock in the front foyer. It was already twenty minutes to five.

"I know you can do it, Harry. But don't rush too much," Mom said as she kissed his forehead. "This contest is important but we don't need you sailing over the handlebars either."

"No worries. I got this."

Harry flew out the front door. He jumped on his ten-speed and pedaled as hard he could down Nightingale Lane.

Harry had many duties at the Moon home

2

like cutting the front and back yards, raking the leaves in fall, shoveling the front sidewalk in winter, keeping the bird feeders filled, and making sure his own bedroom was clean and halfway neat. He also folded the laundry on the uneven days – Monday, Wednesday, and Friday. He and his dad cooked dinner once a week. His sister, Honey, also had chores, although Honey didn't always take her duties as seriously as Harry did. Honey was *expected* to manage the laundry on Tuesday, Thursday and Saturday. She was in charge of the plants – inside and out which meant the fertilizing, too. She was also responsible for the organization of the pantry. The Moons had a pretty good operating system going for them. The household ran like a well-oiled machine most of the time.

Harry's dad preferred to call chores "duty". "It feels more noble," he had said once. "After all, we Moons are all Knights of Nightingale Lane."

"We are?" Honey had asked when she was only eight. "Even girls are knights?"

3

"Yes, even girls," Dad said.

"What about babies, like Harvest? Are they knights?" asked Honey.

"No, Harvest is a knight in *training*," Dad said. "You have to be at least seven. That's when a person has reason and sense. A baby is still figuring things out. So maybe he's a baby knight."

4

"What about a cool knighting ceremony for Harvest when he gets old enough?" asked Harry.

"Maybe. When he's old enough to have duties like you two."

"You mean chores," Honey said.

"They are not chores!" Harry said. "They are *duties*."

"That's because you have been brainwashed," Honey said. "By all those Jedi Knight and King Arthur stories."

"Not at all," Harry said. "I'm a noble guy. I conduct my duties with honor."

"That's the spirit," Dad said.

"That's the spirit of *brainwashing*," Honey had said.

Harry pedaled as fast as he could toward the Post Office. It was another chilly but crisp fall day. It was always autumn in Sleepy Hollow where everyday was Halloween, where every sight and every store and practically every lawn was decked out in honor of the scary holiday. Harry felt a chill wriggle down his spine. And it wasn't from the cool wind. It was the town. Sleepy Hollow had been plunged into a state of eternal Halloween by the evil Mayor Maximus Kligore. He had convinced the townspeople that this plan would bring mountains of revenue into their economy as it became a world-renowned tourist destination. And his evil plan worked. The people loved the idea and embraced Halloween in every way, in every shape, in every nook and cranny of the town. Everyone but Harry. He knew Kligore was planning something much more evil and diabolical for Sleepy Hollow, and Harry was out to stop him. No matter what.

Even as he pedaled, Harry was aware of the feelings deep in his chest. He had learned to pay attention to those feelings with the help of his best friend and nearly constant companion, Rabbit.

"Pedal hard," Rabbit said. "Honey's contest entry cannot be late." Rabbit appeared on Harry's handlebars.

"I know. I'll make it," Harry said.

Rabbit's long, lop ears stood straight up in the wind.

"Waaaahoooo!" Rabbit shouted. "I love the wind on my face. It feels just great to get out in the sunshine!"

"I'll make it," Harry repeated. "But I am pretty surprised that Honey even wrote the essay for the ModBot contest. She's not exactly a tech nerd. I mean, why is it so important to her?"

"I know, it does seem a little out of character—whoaaaaa," Rabbit said as Harry took a hard turn. "Slow down, buddy. Don't want to scrape you off the street."

"Sorry," Harry said. "What time is it, Rabbit?"

"Four-forty-nine. Just enough time to spare," Rabbit said. He never needed to look at a watch or cell phone.

"Rabbit, how do you know like everything?" said Harry, his hair flying under the pressure of the wind. He could see the small post office now. It was tucked between Chillie's Costume Store and the Sleepy Hollow Pharmacy on the other side of the Town Green.

"Let's just say I have been around this block a lot longer than Siri," Rabbit said.

Harry pedaled hard the closer he got to the PO.

"I'm going to jump," he warned as the bike slid on to the lawn outside the Sleepy Hollow Post Office.

"Woo Hoo," Rabbit said. "Rabbits do like jumping."

Harry grabbed his backpack. He and Rabbit ran up the stone stairway to the post office just as Mrs. Brewster turned the "closed" sign on the glass door.

Harry pulled on the door handle. "Nooo! Am I too late? Tell me I'm not too late."

Mrs. Brewster looked at her wristwatch behind the door. "Not by my watch, Harry Moon."

"Thank you, thank you! You saved my life." Harry yelled through the glass.

Mrs. Brewster pushed open the door. "Come on in Harry. You look like you have a postal emergency."

Harry stepped over the threshold with Rabbit at his side. "I do. This needs to be postmarked by five today."

"Don't you worry," said Mrs. Brewster. She was born and raised and lived all her life in Sleepy Hollow and started working at the post office right after high school. Now she was the town's postmaster.

9

Mrs. Brewster stamped the envelope addressed to the Super ModPod Contest organization. She held the envelope up for Harry. "No problem. Sixty seconds to spare."

"Hold that pose," Harry said. "I need to take a picture for Honey so I can prove that I made it."

Harry pulled his phone from his backpack. "Say cheese."

Mrs. Brewster pointed to the postmarked and said, "Cheese," with a wide grin.

Harry texted the image to his mom and Honey. "There ya go," he typed in.

Mrs. Brewster looked at the envelope. "Hmmm," she said, "So Honey entered The Super ModPod Essay Contest."

"Yes, my sister, Honey, but she got the flu and almost missed the deadline...."

"So that's why you are right on time," said

Mrs. Brewster. "Why, I have to admire Honey for her stick-with-it-ness," she said. "And good for her to enter a ModPod contest that is always so identified with boys," she said with a smile. The silver haired grandmother held up her fist in the rally gesture for change. "Girl power!"

"Girl power!" said Harry as he bumped his fist with Mrs. Brewster. He liked Mrs. Brewster. She was always super nice to him and always treated him like an adult.

11

"Modbots are not just for boys, Mrs. Brewster, " said Harry. "They have been making toy sets for girls for years. It's branched off into all kinds of tech. Modbot is like Cisco or Apple. Now it makes all kinds of gadgets for the smart house."

"Smart house?" Mrs. Brewster said. "No thanks. I'll stick with my good old dumb house. I know where everything is and what it will do."

"Awww, nothing can go wrong with the

ModPod. Not with the ModBot people behind it. You can trust their technology."

"Well, that might be so, but no thanks. And I do hope she wins," said Mrs. Brewster. "I do have to tell you, I've seen a lot of envelopes addressed to the contest this week."

"I bet. I figure she doesn't have much of a chance," Harry said. "But thumbs up for trying."

12

Mrs. Brewster looked into Harry's eyes. "That's the point, Harry. Your little sister put it out there. She took a chance. Maybe there will be millions who entered whatever this contest is," she said as she looked at the letter one last time and then put it in the out-bin. "But the important thing is, Honey Moon did it. And you helped make that happen by getting it here in time."

"I guess," Harry said feeling a little ashamed for what he said. "She is a good writer and it *is* an essay contest."

Rabbit tugged Harry's pant leg. "And she has a lot of good ideas."

"And she has a lot of good ideas," Harry repeated.

"There is power in the written word, Harry. The world is changed by words. I am sure that Honey Moon's words, flu or not, have power. And when they go out to a world, it's like your magic, Harry. Honey may just have a different kind of magic. We can change the world with our words. Words are like tiny life rafts that carry the truth. Words that touch hearts."

13

Harry smiled and ran his hand through his hair. "I guess I should have a higher opinion of my sister, after that speech," Harry said as he wiped the sweat off his palms on his jeans. "Don't get me wrong, Mrs. Brewster, I *love* Honey, I just don't *like* her. She's annoying."

"Suck it up, Harry. She's your sister," said Mrs. Brewster. "I know your dad is big on duty, but that's your duty, too. You have to do more than love you sister. You have to find a way to like her."

Harry's phone pinged. He looked at the text.

Thnk u. U R my hero 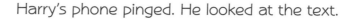!"

He showed it to Mrs. Brewster.

"From my sister. She got the picture of the postmark. See, I'm her hero." Mrs. Brewster looked into Harry's eyes again as though she was searching for something.

14

"Maybe one day, you will let her be your hero," said Mrs. Brewster.

"Well." Harry sighed. "If she deserves it."

"And you're able to see it," said Mrs. Brewster.

"Thanks again, Mrs. Brewster. Have a nice weekend," Harry said.

"You too, Harry. And remember, you don't need a Smart House to have a great life," said Mrs. Brewster. "The great life is with us now."

The sky was now bright with the white and orange ribbons of the setting sun.

Rabbit looked up at the sky. "I liked what Mrs. Brewster had to say about putting it out there."

"How so?" asked Harry as he straddled the bike.

"Even when it seems pointless, putting it out there is what a Nightingale Knight would do. Maybe a fat *chance* is fat with hope, not with cynicism, Harry. In a few hours, that letter will be sailing through those clouds above. Who knows what might happen?" The Harlequin looked into the sky.

15

"But we have to be realistic, Rabbit," said Harry. "Honey is only in fifth grade."

"Being in fifth grade is a good thing. Marvel Modbot may be the chairman of one of the world's largest corporations, but he is a kid at heart. He's the closest thing your generation has to the real Walt Disney."

Harry felt a little puny. His sister had written a whole essay with the flu. "Then, to kid power," he said holding up his fist.

"To kid power!" Rabbit said.

"You coming with me?" Harry asked.

"I'll just fly. You're tired."

"What does tired have to do with anything?" Harry asked. But Rabbit was right. He was pooped from the long bike sprint. "You're spirit. You weigh practically nothing."

"One report says only twenty-two grams," said Rabbit, as he rubbed his pink nose with his front right paw.

"That's old research," Harry said.

"You're right," said Rabbit." But still. Sometimes a kid needs to be alone and take his time."

Just like that, Rabbit disappeared. Harry smiled. He knew very well that even when

Rabbit was invisible he was still with him.

As he peddled down Shopper's Row, Harry thought how Rabbit was right again. There was no rush to get anywhere. The twilight sky was extraordinary. It blushed pink. Evening birds chirped in the trees and fruit bats swooped through the air.

New England small town life was good, and every town and city has its beauty, Harry thought. Feeling magnanimous, Harry's heart stretched wide as he peddled through the fresh air. "Mrs. Brewster is right," he said aloud. "The great life is here now."

18

THE MODBOT ESSAY

"Anyway," Harry said. "Mrs. Brewster said she was very proud of you for putting it out there, despite the odds". Harry had gotten home just in time for dinner. Honey Moon sat across from him. She wore her pajamas and robe and Harry thought she looked a lot better now.

Her nose was not quite as red.

"That's nice," said Honey as she sipped her protein shake. She glared at Harry with her piercing blue eyes. "But what about you, Harry Moon, are you proud of me? Huh? Are you Harry?"

Harry looked at his obnoxious, pajamaed sister and grit his teeth. Why did she need to goad him? He looked at the sacred words that had been stenciled on the dining room wall. Love, peace, kindness. His parents called those words the operating system of their home. Harry zeroed in on the words *self control*. In that instant, Harry whispered to Rabbit for an extra push to keep his talk steady.

"I am so proud of you, Honey, that words fail me," Harry said. "I am especially proud of you doing it when you were so massively sick."

"I wasn't that sick. It's the flu, not malaria," she said. "And why are you being so nice? Is it because I'm sick?"

Harry shoved a forkful of mashed potatoes into his mouth and shrugged. Sometimes it was interesting to leave Honey wondering.

"I mean writing that essay beat watching daytime television. I did a lot of research. And I'm going to win."

Harry's little brother pushed his sippy cup off his highchair tray and giggled. Honey retrieved it and set it on the tray. "Don't you agree, Harvest? I'm gonna win the contest."

"Win," Harvest said. And Honey smiled.

"I just happen to have a copy of the essay right here," Dad said.

"Where did you get that?" asked Honey.

"I printed out another copy," Mom said. "I wanted your daddy to have the chance to read it."

22

"First of all," Dad Moon said. "I was very impressed, Honey. It is written with intelligence and with heart." He reached across the table and gently touched his daughter's cheek with affection. "If it's alright with you, Honey, I thought I would share with the family a paragraph I found most insightful."

"Of course." Honey smiled. She glared at Harry. "I'm sure Harry would LOVE to hear it."

Harvest clapped.

Harry almost spit mashed potatoes across the table.

"It would be delightful if *daddy* would read to us," Harry said.

"Of course it will be delightful," Honey said.

"Oh brother!" Harry shook his head. "It's just a dumb essay."

"What did you say, Harry Moon? I don't think mom heard you," asked Honey.

"No fighting tonight!" Dad said.

23

"I was thinking, oh brother, what a *lucky brother* I am to be able to hear Honey's essay."

"There is not such thing as luck, Harry. You know that. There is only good fortune and bad fortune. Nothing is random," Dad said.

"The Great Magician has it all in his control."

"If you want, Harry, you could print your own copy," Honey said. "I would be delighted to autograph the winning ModPod essay for you."

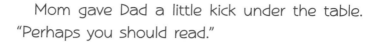

Mom gave Dad a little kick under the table. "Perhaps you should read."

As he cleared his throat, John smiled and looked around the table at his family.

"'Eureka,' by Honey Magdalene Moon," he said.

"Just read that section you found so inspiring, please," said Mom.

24

"In the end, technology can be your best friend," John read, beaming. "But with all best friends, we need to find the right balance in the friendship. Even for those special friends who know everything about us, and love us despite such knowledge, we need to occasionally find some distance. Not every walk, not every conversation, not every meal should be shared with technology."

"If we are going to push forward with innovation, there are those times when we must walk alone, even when it means not taking the hand of our best friend, technology. For as it has been proven in research, the only way to have the "eureka" moment – the advancing thought toward inspiration – is in the solitary walk when are left alone with ourselves to bask in the beautiful cathedral of solitude.

"Scientific research has revealed that the Eureka moment – the immediate discovery of the big idea – occurs in relaxation, not at the desk. This is when the left and right side of our brains are speaking the special language of exalted consciousness. This is the place where wonder happens. Where the big ideas are born. This is Marvel-land. This was so for Archimedes, Einstein, Marie Curie, Edison, Steve Jobs, George Lucas, even the Beatles with their beautiful lyrics. This is surely the way it will be for the innovators of tomorrow. That's what our best friend technology affords us – the time to walk alone and be inspired. Technology gives us the time to dream a future world, a fair and just world for everyone."

John Moon looked up from the paper.

"Wow!" said Mom. "That is written so well, Honey."

25

"Thank you, mommy!" Honey said. She pulled herself up as tall as she could.

"And I do believe it," Dad said, "All of us have to find the right balance in our daily lives and our tech life. Families must learn to unplug together. Go outside, enjoy the fresh air."

"Well, that's not really the point, daddy," Honey Moon said as she munched green beans.

"I think that had to be more than one paragraph, pops," said Harry Moon, talking over his sister. "That was pretty long for only one paragraph, wasn't it? How long was that? Sounded like the entire paper."

"I should have said the end," John Moon interjected. "You're right, Harry. It was more than a paragraph. To be concise, it was the end of the essay which looks to be officially three paragraphs. So yes, Harold, I did read more than one paragraph."

"Whether one or three, what did you think of it, Harry?" Honey asked. "Did you think it had a certain *PHD* flare?"

"It sounded very grown up," Harry said. "I mean, you don't speak like you write."

"Thank goodness for that!" Honey said laughing. "I had to *write up* as they say. The essay jurors are all PHDs and total experts, after all. I just focused my language and thinking to them."

"Why couldn't you just be yourself?"

"It is myself, just with better words. Admit it, Harry, I just blew your mind!" she said.

"Eureka!" he said, trying his best to remain cheery and likeable, although it was a struggle, even with the help and encouragement of Rabbit.

"Honestly, Honey, no joke, "said Harry. "That was pretty impressive. I'm not blowing smoke, either."

Honey relaxed. "Huh." It wasn't often she got a nice compliment from her brother.

"Oh oh," said Harvest.

"What is it, sweetie?" asked Mom.

Harvest puffed out his cheeks and gagged in his throat.

"He's gonna blow!" Harry shouted. "It's the flu. BACK AWAY EVERYBODY!"

"Eureka!" Dad said.

WATCH THE SKIES!

At first, it appeared to be an alien invasion. Like a strange, circus parade from another planet, formidable objects sailed through the grey Sleepy Hollow sky. It had been three months exactly since Harry and Rabbit mailed Honey's essay. Harry had even forgotten about the whole thing.

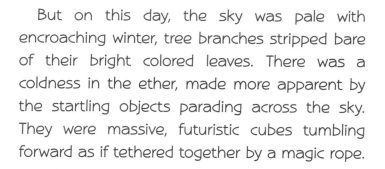

But on this day, the sky was pale with encroaching winter, tree branches stripped bare of their bright colored leaves. There was a coldness in the ether, made more apparent by the startling objects parading across the sky. They were massive, futuristic cubes tumbling forward as if tethered together by a magic rope.

A crowd gathered in the green. Even Mildred Middlemarch, the reporter for the local paper was there watching.

As the alien parade grew closer overhead, Mrs. Middlemarch opened her mouth as wide as a fry pan. Harry gave her a nudge. "It's okay," he said. "I . . . I think."

"What the heck?" she said finally. There had never been anything like this in Sleepy Hollow. "I have got to follow this lead!" she said. "It will make a great story."

Everyone was pointing and chattering about what could possibly be happening.

The circus procession marched high in the

sky above the town square, heading North, past the Headless Horseman statue and the brick clock tower. At the end of the high-flying train was a sleek, shiny glass-like structure, sparkling with the light of faraway stars.

"Who's with me?" shouted Mrs. Middlemarch, as she climbed into her truck. "Let's follow that thing!" she shouted. Sure enough, many from the square stopped what they were doing and jumped into their vehicles. Cars and trucks gunned their engines and headed north in pursuit of the strange, elusive parade traveling high above.

31

The Good Mischief Club of Harry, Bailey, Hao, and Declan stood gazing into the sky.

"What the heck?" Hao said. "Flying saucers! Look!"

"It can't be real saucers," Harry said. "It's got to be a . . . a joke or something."

"It looks like they're headed to Herman

Melville field!" Bailey shouted.

"Follow those saucers!" Hao shouted.

The guys jumped on their bikes and took off toward the field.

Harry kept his eyes peeled on the sky as much as he could. He saw that each of the parade pieces were dragged by a hovercraft – a drone-like helicopter.

32

"Whatever it is, it's making a delivery!" shouted Harry.

"Why are they going to the field?" shouted Declan. "It's empty. There's nothing there!"

"Where else to unload their weapons?" called Hao. The wind whipped his hair back from his forehead as he clutched the handlebars. "They need plenty of room to assemble their weapons of mass destruction! Plenty of space to set up their trajectory to launch rockets into Boston!"

Harry pedaled hard and fast as the strange

parade sailed over his head. The landscape looked especially forlorn against the bare branches of December, reaching high against the lifeless, granite sky. He could barely see the flying saucers on the dusty grey horizon.

"Look! Whatever it is, it's landing!" Harry shouted.

As they turned onto Witch Broom Road, the guys were joined by a row of fast moving cars and trucks, all approaching Herman Melville Field. Harry heard the sound of fire sirens. Sleepy Hollow Engine Five, it's red light whirling, was blasting down Witch Broom Road, past all the cars that had pulled over to the side when the siren was sounded. Like a storm hunter in pursuit of a whirling tornado, Officer Ortiz's parole car chased after Fire Engine Five.

"Whoa! Big stuff going down," said Hao. "I wonder if they have called the National Guard. They always call them as back up in the alien movies!"

33

Harry and his friends slowed as they neared the other vehicles in the middle of the field.

"The hovercrafts are gathering!" Harry shouted.

"This is unbelievable," Declan said as he jumped from his bike. "This is really happening! It's like something out of a sci-fi flick!"

A wintry, gray mist shrouded the strange vehicles. Still, the center of the noise was evident. Harry walked through the noisy crowd – there were people of all ages, from great grandparents to toddlers, from farmers, shop keepers, moms, and Mildred Middlemarch. She was ready for anything. She held her phone in one hand and her pencil and pad in the other.

"What do you make of this, Mrs. Middlemarch?" Harry asked.

"I was hoping you'd tell me, Harry Moon. You are the magic man around here," she said, her eyes glued to the grey sky.

"This is not magic. This is tech at an extremely high order," Harry said as he watched the sky as well.

"Interplanetary?" she asked.

"Nahhh. I think from here," he replied. "Earth."

"I think not. They are controlling the weather. Look at this field, Harry Moon! They have brought in the fog so we humans can't see the mothership."

35

"Or maybe, Mrs. Middlemarch, it's actually just the weather," Harry said.

"I agree with you, Mrs. Middlemarch," Hao piped in. "This obfuscation is tactical. In Star Trek, the ships are always putting up their invisible shields so that the dark side can't discern the ship's maneuvers."

Harry rolled his eyes. "Obfuscation?" He punched Hao's shoulder. "You big goose. You watch way too many sci-fi shows."

The sound from above grew louder still. Through the grey veil above, objects began to appear. Like silver pieces in a steely quilt, patches of platform-like forms lowered themselves from the mist. Harry counted at least twenty shiny cube-shaped pieces hovering in the atmosphere above the field. Onto the level field, the silver platforms dropped. Like beads of mercury on a lab table, the platforms rolled into one another on the ground and formed one massive imprint of silver.

36

"It's code!" Declan whispered. "Some kind of mechanical crop circle!"

"Crop circles use the fields and vegetation to form their messages," Harry said. "This is using architecture."

The crowd watched, captivated as glass and metal gently descended from the mist and assembled onto the silver platform. Mrs. Middlemarch videoed the whole thing. Even against the noise of the machines above, the crowd let out a gasp that could be heard across the field.

"Wait a minute!" shouted Hao, "Did I just see a potted plant?"

"I think you may have," said Harry. "I saw it too."

"This is like Vegas," Bailey said. "Not that I have been to Vegas, but how I would imagine Vegas to be if I actually went to Vegas. You know what I mean."

From the mist, without jetpack or bubble, three silver beings dropped. They appeared cocoon-wrapped in shiny silver pods. They did not float, they shot through the air. Within moments, they arrived inside the rapidly congealing shape of what looked like a single-story space station.

"What the heck?" said Mrs. Middlemarch. "Those are absolutely interplanetary beings. They must be. Are they dangerous?"

"From the looks of Officer Ortiz, they are," said Declan with a snarky clip in his voice. "He looks scared out of his gourd."

Harry turned to see Officer Ortiz, in his standard-issued blue uniform, approaching the mysterious space station. He was all gun. He held his pistol out in front of him as far as he could as he walked.

"Ah, he's just being cautious," said Harry.

"What's with the dinky 45?" said Hao. He snorted. "Ya think that tiny pistol is going to save us against their weapons of mass destruction?"

"Come on," Harry said. "We saw a potted plant fly by, not a terminating transformer."

"Come to think of it," said Bailey, "this station looks a lot like my Modbots."

Harry laughed, then studied the silver, glass monolith before him. Bailey Wheeler was right. The outer-space station looked like it was built from Modbot bricks.

The ear-splitting metal on metal and scraping glass in the sky slowly abated. As the futuristic station settled down on Herman Melville Field, the cacophony from the sky diminished to an eerie silence. Such quietude only heightened the sense of anticipation from the crowd. All eyes were on the glass door at the front of the station.

Harry swallowed. Hard. Like he just swallowed a whole orange. Mrs. Middlemarch inched closer to him. "It's incredible," she whispered. "Is it one of your magic tricks?"

"No," Harry said. "I couldn't do anything like this."

A ramp opened outside the front floor as if by magic. But this was not deep magic, Harry thought, this was the beauty of sophisticated technology.

It was so quiet in the field that as the glass door opened above the ramp, the entire crowd could hear Officer Ortiz cock his pistol.

"Come off it, Ortiz," cried Mildred Middlemarch. "That's a heck of a way to greet

39

the alien visitors! Put that thing down. You will hurt somebody."

Harry agreed, even though he was not convinced that the silver pod astronauts were aliens. In fact, even in the face of potential danger, the assembled crowd of Sleeping Hollow residents agreed with Mildred Middlemarch. To Harry, there was just something about that flying, potted fichus plant that did not settle with an image of galactic warfare.

"Put the gun down, Officer!" said one Sleepy Hollow townie.

"Let's hear what they have to say!" said another.

"We're a spooky town, but we're a peaceful town!" shouted another.

"Let's show our visitors some good ol' Yankee hospitality!"

"But they're trespassing!" Ortiz yelled.

"Of course, they're trespassing. You're always trespassing when you're from another planet!" shouted Hao.

"Look," Harry said. "Someone is coming out."

A young woman, wearing a shiny, silver jumpsuit appeared at the threshold. She moved like a dancer as she passed through the portal. Harry thought she was beautiful. But not as beautiful as Sarah Sinclair, the apple of his eye.

41

"Do not fear!" the woman shouted. "We come in peace!"

A second being appeared behind her. He was sturdy and broad shouldered with a grin plastered across his humanoid face. Any kid might mistake him for Buzz Lightyear. But he was a different kind of buzz.

Harry thought Officer Ortiz looked very small against the large, silver-suited aliens and the big space station. Mrs. Mildred

Middlemarch stepped forward from the crowd to do the talking.

"Visitors, what planet are you from?" shouted Mrs. Middlemarch as she held her tiny mike out to record the answer.

"We are from earth," said the gleaming-toothed, male alien. "But we are from the future!"

The crowd gasped.

Then a silver robot stepped onto the threshold.

"Oh no," Bailey said. "He has a hand cannon. I've seen those in movies. We're all gonna die!"

43

The robot pointed the cannon toward the crowd and pulled the trigger. Screams filled the air as people in the crowd ducked and covered their heads. Tons of colorful confetti shot through the air. The pink, plum, red, and blue flecks flew high into the grey sky, and produced a glistening rainbow.

Music blared through the invisible speakers of the space station. The robot shot the cannon again and this time, a flag unfurled from his blaster.

Then Harry saw him. A living legend. Harry and his friends gulped. From inside the glass threshold walked the great inventor of the Modbot bricks and pathfinder to the future, Mister Marvel Modbot, himself, also dressed in the tight, silver jumpsuit like the others.

"I cannot believe it!" Declan panted. "Is that really Marvel Modbot? Or is that a hologram?"

44

"What a genius!" Bailey said, "But that suit is making him look a little like a metal sausage, yeah?"

The woman alien took center stage. In an instant, her silver glove elongated and transmorphed into a megaphone like the ones cheerleaders use at pep-rallies. She stood at the edge of the space station and addressed the crowd clearly. At this point, pretty much everybody in the crowd was videoing the excitement.

"People of earth," the woman shouted. "I am Talia Fetching. Do not be afraid. I present to you the chairman of Modbot Inc., the one and only

Marvel Modbot, friend to all!"

The too-tight silver jumpsuit, which made him look somewhat ridiculous, added to Mr. Marvel Modbot's charm. He always seemed game for fun and horseplay, even if it made him look downright silly. Harry had grown up watching Marvel Modbot on TV.

Marvel used to host the animated show, *The Marvelous World of Modbots*, which promoted the *Create-Your-Own-Modbot* product line. A shrewd businessman, Marvel Modbot was just a big kid. He had a train at his house in Hawaii that you could sit on and ride all the way down to the ocean.

"This is outrageously unbelievable!" Harry said. "Marvel Modbot is standing right here. In Sleepy Hollow. I can't stinking believe it."

It was rumored that Marvel got the name "Modbot" because he was a wild child raised by experimental robots in Silicon Valley. According to the story, the mama-robot exclaimed, "What a Marvel!" when she first

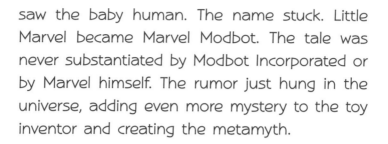

saw the baby human. The name stuck. Little Marvel became Marvel Modbot. The tale was never substantiated by Modbot Incorporated or by Marvel himself. The rumor just hung in the universe, adding even more mystery to the toy inventor and creating the metamyth.

Marvel waved to the crowd as the applause rose across the field. He smiled. His bright, white teeth glistened. After all, he had been on TV. He knew the moves to capture hearts, but as Harry Moon watched him, Harry sensed Marvel's goodness wasn't just for show. He radiated it.

The townies in Herman Melville Field screamed with such vigor that for several minutes, Marvel Modbot could not get a word out. Finally, the other costumed alien took control of the town's frenzy. He morphed his silver helmet, framing his head into a massive high-tech speaker.

"Please, everyone," he shouted. "My name is Buzz Goodmorrow."

The crowd cheered and whooped and whistled. Buzz raised his hands. "Silence! Marvel Modbot has an important message for you. Sleepy Hollow, Massachusetts is in for a big surprise!"

The crowd went wild again. Following some random honking of truck and car horns in anticipation of Marvel's "surprise", the crowd calmed down to listen.

"Thank you, good people of Sleepy Hollow," Marvel said. "As you know, I am a believer in America's children. They are our greatest treasure. In our children resides our hope in a better future – free of war, free of worry, and filled with the opportunity for all citizens to enjoy the beauty of life. Even with all its ups and downs, I still believe that life is beautiful."

There was further applause at Marvel Modbot's encouraging words.

"I have two wonderful announcements to make to you today here at the historic Herman Melville Field."

47

Another round of cheers and applause.

"I still can't believe it," Harry said. "What could Marvel Modbot possibly have in store for Sleepy Hollow? It's already Spooky Town."

"Yeah," Bailey said. "What in the world?"

"One thing for sure. Whatever it is, I don't think Mayor Kligore is gonna like it," Harry said.

"As I said, I am a believer in America's Children," continued Marvel. "Today, I am here, on behalf of Modbot Incorporated to honor a particular child. Yes, friends, my company conducted an essay contest on using technology responsibly. The winner of the contest is from the fifth grade of Sleepy Hollow Elementary School, Miss Honey Moon, age ten!"

Harry's mouth dropped in surprise as his buddies slapped him on the back. He was related to her, after all. Harry looked around. But he didn't see Honey or his parents anywhere. Then he remembered. They had gone into Boston to do some shopping.

"The winning prize," Marvel shouted, "is a weekend stay in our Marvelous Modbot ModPod! Honey Moon and the Moon family will experience the first ever Marvel Dream Experience! They will live in high-tech luxury, a burden free life in the marvelous, fully integrated, smart house that includes the latest in 3D printers. The ModPod is so forward in its design and execution, that our logo, "'If you dream it, we will build it,' finally comes true."

Harry covered his ears when Mrs. Middlemarch let out a cheer so loud he thought she could have caused an avalanche.

49

"My associate," Marvel said, "Buzz Goodmorrow, is correct when he told you that we come from the future and we do, through the door of the amazing Modbot ModPod! The future is here, friends of Sleepy Hollow. But, as I said, I have a second announcement this fine day."

Always a showman, like Harry, Marvel Modbot knew how to hold an audience. He stood silently at the top of the shining ramp in front of the coolest, most space-age

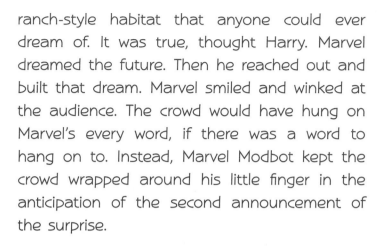

ranch-style habitat that anyone could ever dream of. It was true, thought Harry. Marvel dreamed the future. Then he reached out and built that dream. Marvel smiled and winked at the audience. The crowd would have hung on Marvel's every word, if there was a word to hang on to. Instead, Marvel Modbot kept the crowd wrapped around his little finger in the anticipation of the second announcement of the surprise.

50

"Now, that's a different kind of magic," said Harry to Bailey, Declan and Hao.

"What's that?" asked Bailey.

"How he holds the audience in the *Sleight Of Hand*. He's disorienting them with his silence. They might as well be in outer space. Then, he'll masterfully land them in their wanderings with the announcement. It doesn't matter what it is. They will be grateful to be grounded. Smokes. Marvel Modbot is a genius."

"How do you know all that?" Bailey asked.

"He's a magician, dummy," Hao said, breaking

into the conversation. "He's trained to know these things when you learn the magic of *Sleight of Hand*."

Marvel Modbot spoke. "So my friends, all of us who grew up in small town America know that moms and dads matter most to a child. But it takes a town to raise a hero. When I read Honey Moon's touching essay about how we must have the free time to hear ourselves think, to find our 'Eureka moment', I knew, at once, that Honey Moon had more than mom and dad behind her. She had all of Sleepy Hollow. Of course, I know how New England Governance runs, and so a vote of support will need to be made by a Town Meeting. If you will honor me by accepting my gift, then I will honor you. The Modbot Foundation is now fully prepared, by the vote of its board, to retrofit Sleepy Hollow, Massachusetts with all the latest tech, at Modbot's expense, making this wonderful place America's first fully integrated "Smart Town".

The crowd gasped. People hooted, hollered, and honked their car horns. For a

51

second time, Mrs. Mildred Middlemarch's mouth dropped. Her lips formed an "OMG", rounding even wider than a fry pan.

When Mrs. Middlemarch finally could speak, she exclaimed, "Harry Moon, this is the story of the decade, the story of the century! This can't wait! I'm going to print today."

"Get on it, Mrs. Middlemarch!" Harry said.

"You got it, kid!" She dashed to her truck.

"Wow!" said Harry to the Good Mischief Club, "I have to tell Honey and Mom and Dad."

"Yeah," Hao said. "It's a shame they aren't here."

"We're gonna live in SMART TOWN!" cried Declan. He was thrilled with the news, jumping up on Bailey, grinding his knuckles into his head with a noogie. "Someone pinch me!" Declan shouted.

"How about I throttle you instead?" Bailey asked.

MOVE OVER

"Move over? screamed Mayor Maximus Kligore. "Move over?" The mayor sat at his large, baronial desk at the We Drive By Night Company, fuming. Clutching the latest edition of *Awake In Sleepy Hollow*, he growled at the banner headline. "No one's moving anywhere!"

He was shouting so loudly that his office assistant, Miss Cherry Tomato, in her too-tight red dress and Jimmy-Choo heels, dashed into the office.

"Boss Man! What's wrong, Boss Man?" she asked, her face as flush as the red fruit after which she was named.

"This is what's wrong, Miss Tomato!" Mayor Maximus Kligore shouted, slamming the paper down on his big desk.

Miss Tomato leaned over the desk and read the large black and white banner to the local paper. She could read some, but she really did not believe in reading.

"*Move over Spooky Town, Here Comes Smart Town,*" Cherry Tomato recited from the headline. "So what's the big deal, Boss Man?"

"Read on, Cherry," Mayor Maximus Kligore.

"Now, you know I do not like to read. 'Ignorance is bliss', as they say," she said.

"READ!" Kligore snarled.

"A technological revolution has landed in our town of Sleepy Hollow in the form of the Modbot ModPod," she read carefully and slowly. "If Town Meeting approves of a new tech-restoration plan to be outlined tonight by billionaire visionary, Marvel Modbot, Sleepy Hollow will become the first completely integrated smart town in North America."

55

Cherry Tomato looked across the desk at the mayor. With his clenched fists and grimacing face, he appeared ready to explode. "Will someone PLEASE tell me, Miss Tomato, how Marvel Modbot landed a dang-huge ModPod on Herman Melville Field WITHOUT MY PERMISSION!?"

"Boss Man, I do not know," she said, sheepishly.

"And how did the matter of the Modbot Tech Restoration get on tonight's Town Meeting agenda without me approving it?" he asked.

"Boss Man, you do not approve the meeting agenda, the people's elected Selectmen do," said Cherry Tomato.

Kligore fumed even more. His temples pounded as he spoke. "In reality, it is I who rules this town. Never ever forget that, Miss Tomato. I also rule this office, so I want answers, answers, Miss Tomato. Chase down the truth, Miss Tomato. Hunt it down, NOW! Get back to me, SWIFTLY! As it does not involve reading, but digging in the dirt, you should be able to accomplish that simple duty in DUE HASTE!"

"On it, Boss Man," Cherry said. She backed out of the room. She knew when the mayor got angry, it was best to simply get right to work.

She clicked in her heels over to her desk and grabbed the phone, and started punching in numbers. She talked to old Lander Walker, the thin and elderly Deputy of Permits and Trash for the town. She spoke to Candace Smith, head of the five-member board of Selectmen, the executive arm for most New England Towns. New England governance, including Sleepy Hollow governance, much to the chagrin of the power-hungry Mayor Maximus Kligore, consisted of three arms: the mayor, the Selectmen, and the town in the form of "Town Meeting".

Mayor Kligore held his head in his hands as he stared at the paper. He believed he ruled Sleepy Hollow by his fiery darkness. But he also knew the truth. He couldn't control everything. He didn't like it, but he knew it. That being said, Kligore also knew how much he influenced Sleepy Hollow. But some decisions were in the hands of the people. In principal, that is the American way. The government and executive arms, whether in New England or in Washington D.C., are to represent the people, not themselves. They serve in office by "the pleasure of the people". Representatives are voted in to office to represent their constituents. Every four years, even Mayor Kligore's position in Sleepy Hollow, must be voted upon. By his filthy leadership and help from the dark side, Mayor Kligore always won reelection and Sleepy Hollow had become a vital and successful tourist town by rebranding itself as *Spooky Town where Every Day is Halloween.*

But. Kligore hated not having total control.

Miss Cherry Tomato finished her investigation on the phone, and dashed into the Mayor's office to report back to Kligore. Miss Tomato's whole demeanor changed. She was happy as a lark. With enthusiasm, she launched into her report. "All of Sleepy Hollow is buzzing with excitement, Boss Man," she said happily.

"Wow. Well, that's exactly not what I asked, Cherry. I want to know how that blasted ModPod got into the town without a permit. How did this Marvel Modbot issue get on the Town Meeting agenda? And why wasn't I asked?"

"Of course, Boss Man, " said Cherry Tomato, as she glanced over her note pad. "Easy Peasy. Mrs. Delores Wyatt in Lander's office approved the permit for Melville Field. She said the Modbot company did everything on the straight up, Boss Man. The permit is for today through Monday and it was under the,..." she said, trailing off for a moment as she scouted for a detail, "...oh, here it is. The permit was granted under 'Public Exhibition Code 92r'. It's all legal beagle, Boss Man. As for the Selectmen approval for Mr. Modbot to speak at Town Meeting tonight, I spoke with Candace Smith and she filled me in. She said and I quote, 'the Board of Selectmen is intrigued but undecided on the proposal to bring a technologically advanced system into the hollow. However, it is not often that a chairman of a major American company offers to speak to a small

town, so we have allowed it'. End quote."

Kligore rose from his leather chair. Miss Cherry Tomato watched her boss. She knew what he was doing in quiet moments like this. He was checking his evil gut. He reached across the desk and grabbed his glass of water. He guzzled it down like his life depended on it. Cherry looked on, mesmerized by her idol.

"Thank you, Miss Tomato. I see this war has only begun," he said.

"What war, Boss Man?" she asked.

"There is much confusion in the world, Miss Tomato. There is a lot of noise in the marketplace. It is hard to get traction. It is difficult to be special in the commercial arena. Sleepy Hollow has risen above the trash with the brand *Spooky Town*. We have turned the tide. Sleepy Hollow has become successful. If the town strays from the brand into a tech brand, there is only confusion. Doesn't the Bible say that a house divided will not stand?"

"Boss Man, you know I do not read," Miss Tomato replied.

"That's what it says, alright. I do read," said Mayor Maximus Kligore as he breathed deeply, puffing up his chest. She noticed that he towered over his desk. Miss Cherry Tomato laughed nervously. She could feel Boss Man's power. It was as if her report and the water had rejuvenated him, even transformed him.

"Why are you laughing, Miss Tomato? Are you laughing at *ME?!*" he roared.

"No, no, Boss Man," she said quickly. "I ain't laughing at you. I'm laughing at the idea of you sitting in your chair reading that big, black leather book. It tickled my funny bone, Boss Man, that's all." She smacked her gum. "I mean, why on earth, Boss Man, would you read a book like *THAT?!*"

"Miss Tomato, you have so much to learn. But I can teach you."

"Thank you, Boss Man."

"I read the Bible so I can put the dark twist on it. Use the words to my advantage. Watch me, tonight, at Town Meeting, Miss Cherry Tomato. And be afraid."

"Okay, I will," she said.

"That's the way we work at the We Drive By Night S Corp, Miss Tomato. We mix our lies with the truth. We confuse the goodness of people. In the dark twist, they grow lost. They become ours."

62

"Wow! I guess I should read more."

"Miss Tomato, you do not read at all."

NERVES

That afternoon Honey received the most incredible phone call of her life. It was from Marvel Modbot himself. As she listened to him tell her she won the contest it felt like her entire body had been zapped with lightning. She could hardly stop shaking from excitement and nerves.

THE SCARY SMART HOUSE

"I can't believe it," she said into her Mom's cell phone. "Really? I really won?"

"You sure did, Honey," Marvel said. "Your essay was excellent."

Honey felt tears well up in her eyes. Mom stood close with a box of tissues.

"Thank you," Honey said. "Thank you and yes, I will tell my parents everything you said."

She clicked off the phone, let go a huge sigh and fell into her mother's embrace. "I won, Mom," Honey said. "I won."

Mom stroked Honey's hair. "You did. I am so proud of you."

Honey pulled away and looked her Mom in the eyes. "We've been invited to dinner tonight. With . . ." Honey had to take a deep breath she was so excited. "With Marvel tonight."

Honey explained the rest of the details. "And the best part is that we get to live in the Smart House for the whole weekend. The whole family."

Later that evening the Moon Family were getting ready for their dinner with Marvel Modbot. Becky and Brianna helped Honey dress for the most important night of her life. Becky was in charge of Honey's hair. For three hours, Becky had been fine-braiding Honey's hair so she could look like the fairy-princess, Reanna, who reigned over the Modbot

65

theme parks. She gathered Honey's fine hair at the back of her neck and plaited into a waterfall of braids and curls woven with tiny, silk blue-bell flowers. It was work that required focus, along with a few squeaks and yelps from Honey when Becky pulled too tight.

Meanwhile, Brianna was in charge of Honey's dress, shoes, and clutch bag. The hem had come undone on Honey's dress when their dog, Half Moon, plowed into the room and caught the dress on one of his pointy toe nails. Honey screamed, "Get out. Get out, you clumsy animal." But hemming a dress was easy for Brianna.

That was when Honey decided to move the hair-braiding operation into the bathroom. They had been in there almost an hour when they heard a knock on the door.

"Can a guy get in there to comb his hair?" Harry shouted.

"Not unless he wants to get his hair braided like Princess Reanna!" shouted Becky as she turned her eyes to Honey. "I'll take him on. He doesn't scare me!"

66

"He doesn't scare me, either," said Honey with a laugh. "I think that's the problem."

"Come back later!" shouted Brianna.

"Kill me now," Harry sighed as he walked away from the bathroom. Harry was used to ruling the roost at Nightingale Lane. He was the Big Kahuna. The top dog. He was magic man. He really did not need a princess of words messing with his dominion.

Becky finally finished Honey's hair. Honey stood in front of the mirror and practically swooned. "Wow, she said. "It's spectacular. I look just like Princess Reanna."

"All you need is the dress. I'm sure Brianna is finished with it by now."

"This is your night, Honey Moon! It's like going to prom!" said Brianna as she tied the thread at the hem.

"Kinduh," Honey said as she pulled the flowing dress over her shoulders. "But better. Much, much better."

67

"You know what I learned from Rabbit?" Harry asked as he sat on a bench in his mom and dad's bedroom, combing his hair with his dad's brush. Harry was already dressed in a button-down shirt and slacks. He watched his mom at the mirror straighten her strand of crystal beads given to her by their dad for their fifteenth wedding anniversary.

"What did you learn, Harry?" Mary Moon asked.

"I learned the way to read. You have to bring your whole self to reading. That means your heart, body, mind and soul – to the words. Rabbit helps me read, helps me be discerning. People twist words all the time. But when I read with my wholesome self, I see the truth behind the words. Does that make sense, mom?"

"Yes, Harry," she said, picking up a perfume atomizer and giving her neck and ears a spritz. "Do you know at Harvard that the original shield of the University had three books spelling out

Veritas or Truth? On the shield, two books are open upwards, signifying the knowledge that students can learn on their own. The third book is turned down, flat against the table. That book of knowledge is available only through the eyes of the soul. Did you know that Harry?"

"No," Harry said. "That's pretty cool."

"In other words," Mom added. "There are certain deep understandings that can only be attained not through the mind alone. And that was at Harvard, Harry!"

69

"So I have a point to my story," Harry said.

"What is the point?" asked Dad as he opened the bathroom door and entered the bedroom. He was dressed in a white shirt and tie.

"Wow, Dad," said Harry Moon. "It's not even Sunday."

"Not everyday we get an opportunity to

have dinner with the toy tycoon of the world!" he said smiling.

"You clean up nice, Dad," Harry said.

"Not bad for a nerd," Mom said.

"My point to the story might strike you both as out of character," Harry said. "But when I read Honey Moon's essay, I really tried to read it with all of me including the Rabbit part."

"Okay," said Mom as she walked from the mirror and took her jacket from the bed. "Hit us up, Harry Moon. What did you learn?"

"It was almost a miracle, I think. I mean, as I read it, I thought, 'gee, Honey is not so bad after all.'"

"Haven't we been telling you that, son? For how many years now? You must love your little sister," said Dad.

"I do love her, dad. I don't like her. She has a grating, extremely annoying laugh." Then he mocked her with its sound. "He-haw-ho-haw-he-haw," he said as he shivered with his own mimicry.

"I think it's more like a giggle," said Mom.

"That's the point, I guess. When I read her Eureka essay, I said to myself, 'gee, I like this writer. I would like to get to know her.'"

"She's right across the hall, sweetie," said Mom. "You can get to know her now by telling her to meet us at the car."

"Get your sister," Dad said. "She must be ready by now. I don't want to be late. Mrs. Wilcox is already with Harvest. No need to lock up." Dad straightened his tie.

"You clean up nice, too," Harry said.

Harry knocked on Honey's door. "Honey, it's me."

"What do you want?" said Becky through the closed door.

"We need to leave. Can I come in?"

"I suppose," Honey said.

Harry opened the door and looked at his kid sister who at that moment looked much older than ten years old. She wore a red and plum floral dress with plum flats. The shiny shoes sparkled like fairytale shoes. Honey's blonde hair was plaited on the sides, away from her face. As she turned around for her older brother to see all of her, Harry noticed that she looked like a fairy princess in the Princess Reanna movies.

"Wow!" said Harry. "You look terrific, sis."

Honey beamed from the compliment. Even her grid of silver braces shined. Brianna and Becky stood behind Honey like the princess' ladies in waiting.

"Becky braided my hair. Mom even let me have a dab of her perfume."

"Great work, girls," Harry said with a sigh.

"We got to go," Harry said. "Mom and dad are already in the car."

"Okay," Honey said. She walked to her desk and picked up a small, plum colored clutch purse. It matched her shoes perfectly. Harry was surprised that his little sister was carrying a purse. She usually carried an over-stuffed backpack.

"Mom bought it for me on account of the essay and the dinner. She said it matched my Sunday shoes."

"All grown up." Harry smiled. He even opened the bedroom door wide for Honey. "Chivalry is not dead."

"Whoa," she said. "What's gotten into you?" Honey asked as she crossed the room to the open door. "Holding the door and everything for me. I'm not the real Princess Reanna."

"Tonight, you are," Harry said. As Honey passed him with her fairy-styled hair and her fancy shoes, Harry stopped her with a hand

83

on her arm. "I wanted to tell you something," he said.

"What?" she asked.

He turned his eyes to Becky and Brianna.

"And your girl-power gang can hear it, too. I learned a lot from your essay. That whole thing about Eureka and how inspiration comes when you least expect it. That was powerful stuff. When I was reading it, I thought you are a really great writer."

"So what are you saying? You not only love me, but you like me?" she said as she walked out of her room.

"Something like that," Harry mumbled.

MEETING MARVEL

The ModPod people had arranged dinner at the swanky and upscale Haunted Wood Brasserie. The restaurant was "ol fashioned wow" according to Hao Jones. The Haunted Wood used freshly laundered and pressed white table cloths and silver candelabras. In fact, the Moons never ate there because it was simply too pricey for a family of five. But tonight, they were the guests of Mr. Marvel Modbot.

"I still can't believe I won," Honey said as the Maitre D' escorted them to their reserved table.

"Me either," Harry said.

It was like he had forgotten all the nice stuff he had just said and turned back into the same old Harry Moon.

The family sat at the restaurant's best table. It had a view of the Town Green and the Headless Horseman statue which was lit for night, making it possible for tourists to take night photos. Honey shivered when her eyes locked onto the gruesome rider. "Can't it NOT be Halloween for just one night?" she asked.

"Nope," Harry said. He pulled a breadstick from a fancy, crystal vase. "I'm surprised Kligore even let this whole thing go down in his town."

"It's not his town," Dad said. "But I see your point."

Honey felt a check in her spirit. She usually felt some kind of nudge or check when something was not quite right or noble. But tonight she chose to ignore it.

"I just won't look at it," she said.

"Look," Mom said. "We can change seats and you won't be able to see the statue."

John tapped his glass with his butter knife. "Attention Nightingale Knights. I would like to raise a toast to Honey Moon."

Everyone raised their glasses. Mom and Dad had champagne, Honey and Harry each raised their glasses of Pepsi, a rare treat for them both.

"We are so incredibly proud of you Honey. I never had a doubt that you wouldn't be the winner of the ModBot contest. You wrote an outstanding essay."

"She certainly did." It was Marvel Modbot who had just arrived. "I'm sorry I'm late but

I had to speak at Town Meeting." He took the seat next to Honey. She smiled so wide she thought her face would crack.

Without his Marvel Modbot suit, he looked pretty normal, except for a strange glint in his eye. He had a mane of snow white hair and large, almost cartoon-sized spectacles. Harry and Honey found the elderly billionaire to be not only smart, but funny, too. Mr. Marvel Modbot had no trouble expressing himself. Dressed in his suit, he wore his legendary "Glass Bowtie". Marvel was famous for the bowtie. Indeed, the iconic tie harkened back to the story of Cinderella. "Every person on this blessed earth is special," Marvel Modbot had famously said. "We are all Cinderellas or Cinderfellas. The glass slipper and the glass tie are there for everyone. That's why I wear the glass bowtie. To let people know that we all have magic when we treat one another as equals."

Harry was amazed that the old guy actually wore the glass bowtie in real life and not just for the TV show.

"I just thought it was a marketing gimmick," said Harry, respectfully.

"It is no gimmick, Harry," Mr. Modbot replied. "I don't wear my heart on my sleeve. I wear it around my neck."

"Is it real glass?" Honey asked. As the guest of honor, Harry's little sister sat right next to the celebrity tycoon.

"It sure is," Marvel Modbot said. "Check it out, Honey." One of the world's richest men leaned over to Honey and stuck out his collar. She pinged the bow-tie.

Tinnnnng!

"It really is glass," she said.

"Just like a fairy tale. But at Modbot we try to make the tale real."

"That is so cool, sir," Harry said. "What about when you play rugby? I mean, are you still playing rugby?"

"I sure am!" he said, laughing. "Then, I wear a silicone replica. At eighty, I remain formidable, and I remain safe."

"Sir, may I ask you a personal question?" Harry asked.

Mom stepped in. "Now, Harry," she gently chided.

"Oh, it's fine, Mary. I have no secrets," Mr. Marvel Modbot said.

"Maybe you do, sir, " said Harry as he looked across the table at the billionaire.

"Hit me up," Marvel replied. Then he took another spoonful of his chowder.

"Sir, were you raised by robots in the woods of Silicon Valley?"

Once he had finished swallowing his chowder, Mister Marvel Modbot looked directly at the eighth-grader. Harry somehow knew he was going to answer the question but he was going to take the long way around before he did.

"Harry, I believe in the wonder of technology. Like Honey, I too, imagine that technology can free up human beings to unknown leisure. It is my dream to witness intelligently designed technology freeing people to have more time to care and to love."

Marvel looked to Honey and smiled. "That was genius, Honey, truly. Tech allows us to dream even bigger." With her gleaming wide mouth of teeth and silver, Honey returned the smile. "However, as advanced as personal robotics become," Marvel said, as he looked at Mary Moon, who was pretty much aglow with pride for her daughter, "I do not believe that technology will ever replace the heart of the mother. What is the ancient Jewish proverb? 'God could not be everywhere so he created mothers.'"

"Hey, what about us dads?" said Dad, chuckling, enjoying the relaxing conversation.

81

"That goes without saying," Marvel said with a laugh.

"Are you Jewish?" asked Honey.

Marvel Modbot turned to Honey and smiled. "I will tell you this, Honey. I do not wear my religion on my sleeve or on my collar. I hold it in my heart."

The evening wore on and the conversation seemed to never stop. But before it was over Marvel made another announcement. "I have a very special dessert planned."

The Moons all clapped and cheered as did the entire restaurant. Honey had been enjoying how the people did their best to remain respectful of her family and Marvel Modbot. But she knew most of them would have loved to get an autograph.

Their server entered the fancy dining room with a plate on flames. There seemed to be a mountain of cake beneath it.

"Wowie zowie," Harry said. "It's on fire."

"I have a very close friend. She is Swedish," said Marvel, his eyes jumping like a kid's. "She called this the 'Treasure Hunt Surprise'. She made it for her family every Christmas morning until the year she died. God rest her soul."

The server placed the flaming mountain in the middle of the table while Marvel laughed. "The Treasure Hunt Surprise is not like the birthday cake," said Marvel. "It can never be blown out by a single pair of lungs, and I don't care if those lungs belong to Hercules Modbot! It takes a whole family to tame this lion. So on three, my new friends, my dear Moon family, let us all pitch in and blow the house down! Honey, will you do the honors on the countdown?"

Honey Moon beamed. Harry was glad to see his sister so happy. Normally, she was just a grump. Then Harry wondered, "Wait a minute, is that what I see, or is she really that way?"

Honey counted "one-two-THREE" at the very top edge of her lungs. With that, Marvel and the Moon Family blew with all their might. In the magic circle of the moment, Harry realized that it was never hard to love a family like this. Loving was easy. It was the liking part that was hard. But in this instant, in the middle of this moment, Harry knew that he really liked them all. He even liked Honey.

Mister Marvel Modbot was right. It took an entire table to bring down the flames of the Treasure Hunt Surprise. But they did it. And the restaurant erupted into loud cheers and applause. The flames were out, revealing the loveliest of mountains. At its summit ran hot cream and chocolate. Marvel took the cake knife and server from the hands of the waiter and cut and served Honey first as the guest of honor. Then he served Mary Moon. Then he served the two guys. Finally, he served himself.

As Harry ate or devoured it, he could taste vanilla and peppermint and ginger and of course, the chocolate. Harry could see that Marvel was choked up, his eyes pooling with liquid. Probably, thought Harry, from all the happy memories over the years of his own family gathered around the Treasure Hunt Surprise.

"So tell me Harry, in answer to your question about whether or not I was raised by a robot, could a robot make this?" asked Marvel. Harry could only half laugh, his mouth full of the delicious cake.

"Not yet!" Harry answered.

85

"But the dessert is called 'surprise' for there is a special treasure found inside. Tonight,

it is for Honey Moon. So Honey, take these special questing spoons and find it in the remaining cake like you were Princess Reanna, herself."

With a smile, Honey pushed her hair from her face and took the two spoons from Marvel Modbot. Carefully, she rummaged through the mountain of chocolate, cake, and cream. "There it is!" she cried. Using the spoons like a pincer, she pulled a gleaming silver envelope from the cake.

"How do I open it?" she asked. The envelope was covered in cake.

Marvel laughed. "As I always say, sometimes you have to get messy to find the fun."

Of course, for Honey, this was a license to do just that. She pulled at the sticky silver bow. She yanked at the silver paper. Then she gently pulled out a silver cameo attached to a silver necklace.

"In the old days, you presented a champion the key to the city," said Marvel in a kindly voice, his eyes twinkling. "Now, we present the champion with the key with a code. Imbedded in the silver is a chip. As you approach the Super ModPod, it will open. If ever there is trouble, simply press the pendant. So welcome, Honey and the Moon Family to the Marvel Dream Weekend Experience! Tomorrow night, the dream begins!"

Honey held up the heart-shaped amulet on the chain and beamed. "Thank you so much, Mister Modbot!"

"Congratulations, Honey. Sometimes excellence of thought and heart just has to be acknowledged!"

88

HEAT IN THE KITCHEN

The instant she reached the minivan Honey realized that the family had forgotten the leftover Treasure Hunt Surprise.

"I'll go get it," she said.

Honey spoke to the maitre d'. "We forgot

the leftovers," she said. "The Treasure Hunt Surprise."

"Oh dear," he said. "I hope you remembered in time. Follow me to the kitchen. It's not every night that a celebrity like Mr. Modbot dines with us. In all the excitement, your waiter must have forgotten it."

"No problem," Honey said.

90

The swanky restaurant had emptied out, and most of the kitchen staff were tidying up or had already left. Only the dessert chef was there, putting the last touches on a tray of peach cobblers and apple crumbles. On the side of the dessert bar was the white plastic container. "That must be it," the maitre d' said. He opened it and showed the cake inside.

"It's a bit of a mess," he said. "But I'm certain it will still delightful to the taste."

"Oh, that's fine, sir. It's for my brother, Harvest. He's only two. He won't care," Honey replied.

"Very well then, may Harvest Moon enjoy," the maitre d' replied. "And congratulations, Honey."

As Honey walked out of the kitchen, she heard and felt the heat of an argument. It was coming from the door to the alley where deliveries were made. She knew both voices. They belonged to her new friend, Mister Marvel Modbot and Mister Maximus Kligore. Something seemed terribly wrong. Ever curious, Honey sneaked to the open door and listened.

91

"I am sorry, mayor," Marvel Modbot said. "I will not withdraw the proposal. I assure you, there is nothing to worry about."

"You do not have my permission for this. A house divided will not stand!" shouted Maximus Kligore.

"Now, there you go, Mayor, twisting the words of the holy book just like you did at the Town Meeting. I will not stand for it. You confused those poor people in Town Meeting. It's as if you put a spell over them."

Honey felt another check in her spirit.

The mayor blustered like a bull. "I am their mayor. There's no magic. This is my town. I rule by receiving their complete trust."

"All they want to do is the right thing," Marvel said. "There is no reason that Spooky Town and Smart Town can not co-exist."

"The right thing is for you to jump into that space pod of yours and take off!"

Honey had heard enough. Clearly, the mayor was mad and Town Meeting had not gone too well for him. Something was messed up, she thought.

On the ride home, she was quiet. Quiet and tired. She thought about telling her parents about what she heard but she didn't. It was almost like she was afraid to say a word.

That night, Honey Moon dreamed. She was Princess Reanna and she reigned over all of Modbot land. Everyone bowed to her exalted name. Harry was her squire. He had to do real chores, like shining her slippers and braiding her hair. When she awoke she thought is was the best dream she had ever had.

At breakfast, she was greeted by a happy Harvest sitting in his booster chair. The remains of the Treasure Hunt Surprise Cake were smeared on his face and tray. Honey thought it was quite odd that Mom let Harvest eat cake for breakfast. But then she saw the banana that Mom must have hidden in the cake for Harvest to treasure hunt.

93

"Did you like it, big guy?" Honey asked.

Harvest grabbed the yellow banana from his tray, thrusting it into the air.

"Wow! That must have been hard to find in there!" Honey said.

At Sleepy Hollow Middle School, the kids were abuzz with the news about the smart house and the up-coming weekend "Dream Experience". Sometimes Harry felt isolated at school. Not this Friday. As he walked through the wave of kids changing classes, he was met with congratulations and friendly whacks on the back. There were only a couple of mean-spirited kids who sneered at him with eyes of envy. One of the school bullies, Frankie Fowlson stopped him and said, "Listen, runt-body, you had nothing to do with this. This was one hundred percent your sister."

"Then I'll just consider myself fortunate. I'm one hundred percent her brother."

Declan Dickinson grabbed Harry by the arm

and hurried him away from Fowlson.

"Leave it be, Harry. Frankie is just jealous. That's the problem with middle school. Everyone is always comparing. You'll be in the smart house this weekend, Frankie will not."

Harry's day pretty much went on without too many hitches. There were some snide remarks from jealous students, but for the most part everyone was thrilled for him and for Honey. But he did get caught watching the clock several times. Harry could not wait for school to end so he could start the weekend in the Smart House.

Mrs. Middlemarch showed up at the Moon house after school. She even brought a bona fide photographer with her. She wanted to interview Honey for a story about her for the *Awake in Sleepy Hollow* newspaper.

Honey had no trouble mugging for the camera or telling about the whole wonderful experience. This was easily turning out to be the best week of her entire life. Now she was

95

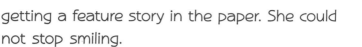

getting a feature story in the paper. She could not stop smiling.

Neither could her Mom who had dashed home early from the hospital after Mrs. Middlemarch called.

"Mister Modbot thought of everything for our family's dream weekend," said Honey as she fingered the silver heart-shaped amulet around her neck. "This special pendant opens up the secrets of the smart house." She smiled brightly for the camera as the photographer clicked away.

As Harry walked into the living room and saw Mrs. Middlemarch and the photographer, he began to backtrack out of the room.

"Just the man I want to see!" said Mrs. Middlemarch as she ran her tape recorder over to Harry.

"So, Harry, what do you think of your little sister winning the Modbot Essay Contest?" With Rabbit's help, Harry managed to shake

96

off his day at school. He seriously didn't want to ruin his sister's moment. Like Rabbit said, "This is Honey's time to shine, not yours."

Truthfully, Harry was more used to being in the limelight than Honey, so maybe it was important for him to be there for her. Help her not to say anything stupid or let it go to her head.

"I am totally pumped over it," Harry said. "I could not be more proud of my sister."

"Oh, Harry!" Honey said. Her thrilled laughter grew into that annoying giggle "he-haw-ho-haw-he-haw" that Harry hated. "That is the nicest thing you have ever said!"

"Okay, let's not wear it out, shall we?" Harry said.

Dad came through the front door and looked into the living room.

"Dad," Honey called. "I'm gonna be in the paper. Mrs. Middlemarch is doing a story. On me. Isn't that spectacular?"

"It sure is, Honey. Spectacular."

Mrs. Middlemarch finished her interview. "It will run in the next edition," she told Honey. "Front page."

MAN IN THE MOON

It was dusk when the Moon family set out for Herman Melville Field. It was quiet except for the hooting owls and the occasional wailing sounds that always seemed to come from Folly Farm. A full moon rose over the cornfields to the east.

"Why do I all of a sudden feel scared?" asked Honey.

"You're just excited, that's all, sweetie," Mom said.

Honey shook her head. "No, I'm scared. Not just nervous. I mean what if something goes wrong? We're in the middle of a field, completely isolated from civilization."

"Our town is civilized?" Harry said in a snarky tone.

"C'mon, Honey," Dad said. "We had dinner last night with one of the nicest guys ever. By reputation, Mister Modbot is very concerned for safety. Besides Buzz Goodmorrow and Talia Fetching are on site if we have any questions."

"Ok, Dad. But I'm still a little scared. I just don't know why."

"Well don't worry, Honey," Mom said. "And we won't be all that isolated. We'll still be in town."

Honey understood that, but still she couldn't deny that check in her spirit she had been feeling. She let go a deep sigh and watched the passing scenery. It wasn't anything she hadn't seen before but tonight it all looked different for some reason. She felt a little better when they passed the Magic Shoppe and she saw Harry's friend Samson Dupree step out of the store and wave. He might be a kook, but he was comforting.

Honey's fears settled into excitement once her Dad pulled the minivan onto the field. The Sleepy Hollow High School Marching Band played *We Are The Champions* as the car pulled toward the house. A Boston news truck had lights and cameras on the Moon Family arrival and there was Mrs. Middlemarch with her phone outstretched taking pictures.

"Feeling better, Honey?" Mom asked as she turned around again to face her daughter.

"Much better!" Honey replied with a big open face, looking at the incredible super-structure before her. It really was a great-looking ranch house. It was all lit up – warm, inviting and modern.

"Is all this for me? It's spectacular." She gave Harry a shot in the arm. "Don't you think it's spectacular Harry?"

Harry only smiled.

"Are you ready with the key to the kingdom?" Dad asked.

Honey fingered the pretty Modbot heart dangling from the silver chain around her neck. She held a large, silver envelope tight in her hand. "I sure am, Dad. Let's go!"

As Honey stepped from the car, the glass door to the house rose like the portal to a flying saucer in those sci-fi flicks. It gave her a chill to see. This was Honey Moon's hard-earned destiny. As the news cameras filmed, Honey slowly walked up the silver ramp as if it was a Hollywood red carpet.

With the music from the band, the warm lights within, all the people, and Buzz Goodmorrow and Talia at the door with flowers for the essay winner, the house out in the

middle of Melville Field did not seem scary anymore.

With her silver amulet around her neck, Honey Moon glided through the portal into the modern house.

The Super ModPod was slick. Buzz and Talia, wearing jeans and Ts, gave a full tour of the house which was impossibly empty of personal things – just white walls. There were no buttons, no switches and no keys.

103

"And don't forget," Buzz said. "The house is totally voice and movement activated. If you want something just ask."

"Wow," Harry said. "It's almost better than magic."

There was the kitchen without visible cabinets or refrigerator, only a white dining table and silicone chairs.

"The best part," Buzz said, "is that once the house learns your thought patterns you

won't even need to ask. Just think."

"Cheerios!" called Harvest standing in the middle of the white kitchen.

Mom and Dad and Talia laughed.

"Look at that," Honey said as a white panel opened, delivering a bowl onto the white counter. Like magic, the bowl zipped down the counter, stopping while another panel opened seamlessly to a Cheerios box which poured the cereal into the bowl. By instinct, Harvest grabbed for it immediately.

"Enough" he said to the cereal box. Instantly, the cereal box disappeared.

The bowl of Cheerios spun over to an invisible refrigerator. The panel lifted to reveal a see-through box of milk gliding toward the bowl.

"No milk, please," said Harvest.

Immediately the milk container stopped.

"Harvest does not need a spoon," Mom said with tinge of nerves.

The drawer instantly shut while the bowl transported itself to the table. Harvest crawled up onto a chair. As he sat on the chair, the seat lifted up six inches to accommodate the toddler's height.

Harvest smiled wide as he grabbed a fistful of cereal.

"That's amazing," Honey said. "My heart is pounding."

105

"Mine too," Harry said. "I can't believe it's happening and I'm seeing it with my own eyes."

"Marvel admires Walt Disney's sense of play," said Talia Fletching. "Of course, Disney once famously said, 'If you can dream it, you can do it.' That's the Super ModPod. As you live in the house, COS will get to know you, and make your dreams come true. The walls are to be filled with whatever you can think of."

"COS?" asked Harry.

"COS is short for Central Operating System," Buzz said. "In this case, COS is tuned in to Honey. She runs the show this weekend as long as she wears the key."

Honey touched the key, making sure it was still there.

"When Honey walks into the house, COS is in full tilt. When she leaves the house, COS goes into sleep mode. There are many layers to the system," said Buzz. "The pod will become busier and fuller once it discovers your likes and interests."

"How so?" Dad asked. "As a computer guy I have to say all this technology makes me very curious."

"For example," Buzz continued. "When Marvel, who is an avid reader, beta-tested the Pod, he dreamed of his heroes. Soon enough, he was not talking to blank walls. He was interfacing with Atticus Finch from *To Kill A Mockingbird*

and Marcus Auerlius, the fair-minded Roman Emperor."

"But where is COS?" asked Harry, looking around.

"C'mon, Moon Family, let's meet COS," Talia said with a smile.

Harry, Honey and the rest of the family followed Buzz and Talia through the white corridors with white carpeting to a white panel at the end of the hallway. Talia motioned for Honey to join her.

As Honey stepped forward, the panel opened. "COS now knows you, Honey. Because of the amulet, COS has been reading your configurations from the moment you put it around your neck at the Haunted Wood Brasserie. He knows your stats, of course, your height, your weight, the color of your eyes – but he also knows your mind. While the amulet has been resting against your collar bone, he has been conducting an in-depth neural scan."

"Wow!" said Honey Moon. "Imagine that. I have become 'Abracadabra'."

Harry shuddered as if she had just giggled.

"Of course, we are here to help and add the 'human touch'," said Talia. "There are all sorts of family filters and protections built into COS."

Talia walked through the threshold of the panel. "Come on in. No worries. COS does not reside in Oz. There are no wicked witches or flying monkeys here."

Honey walked through the portal into the "COS Chamber". The room was shrouded in blue light. In the center of the room a shiny, silver orb, about two feet in diameter, hovered and spun in the middle of the dark room. Once the Moon Family gathered around the sphere, Buzz prompted Honey.

"Honey, why don't you say hello?"

Looking at the faceless orb, Honey shrugged. "Hello, COS, it's nice to meet you."

"It's nice to meet you too, Honey," the orb said. "I hope you and your family have a wonderful weekend here at the house."

Like mist rolling over the earth, a faint layer of information ran over the sphere, congealing into a friendly face.

"Whoa!" Dad said. "Do you recognize him, Honey?"

"No," Honey said. "Who's it supposed to be?"

"That's the first face you ever drew. You were in Kindergarten. I'll never forget that day. You came running into the back yard to show me your Man in the Moon."

110 "That's correct," said the silver orb. But now COS was not some generic silver sphere but bore a child's expression drawn by a child. He bore a grin as wide and thin as the classic *Smiley Face*. The voice no longer was disembodied but sprang from the drawing. "That's the face I found while I configured you," said COS. "You were very happy that day in Kindergarten."

When his back jeans pocket vibrated, Harry pulled out his phone to see a text from Declan. "How's it going in Podville?"

Buzz addressed the happy moon face. "Listen up, COS, this is Honey Moon's family who are here for the weekend. We're expecting

you to give them your best shot."

"Of course, Buzz, there is nothing else but excellence."

Harry texted Declan back. "It's one big crazy dream, bro."

"Let's head back to the kitchen," Talia said.

When they arrived, they sat at the table. "Do you have the bedroom assignments?" asked Talia of Honey.

111

"I do," said Honey. She pulled the silver envelope from under her arm and opened up a blueprint of the house. The house had been customized for the Moon family with bedrooms for everyone.

"Cool," Harry said. "I get my own bathroom. Now that's progress."

"Mom and dad, you take the big bedroom," Honey said as she pointed to the master on the blueprint.

"It's your weekend, princess," Mom said. "You should have the big room."

"There are two of you. There is only one of me," said Honey. "You take the big room."

"That's fine," Talia said. "All the rooms are equipped with the same software."

While she was looking across the table at Harry, she circled the smallest room with her pointer-finger. Then she grinned at Harry.

"Fine with me," said Harry. "I don't mind taking the closet. As Talia said, the rooms all have the same software."

"No, no," Honey said. "That special room is for Harvest."

"You and I will share the rooms of the same size," said Honey. "You pick which one you want, Harry."

"Come on, Honey, It's your weekend. You choose." Harry said.

Honey sat up in her ultra-white chair and put both her palms flat against the table's surface. "Look, everyone," she said. "I am tired of everyone saying it is my weekend. It is just as much Harvest's weekend, or Harry's or Mom and Dad's or Talia's or Buzz's. It doesn't matter who is older or who is younger. Who is brighter or who is stupider. Stupider, is that a word?" She asked as she laughed. "It is your weekend. It is my weekend. It is our weekend! Now, let's be the Nightingale Knights and all for one and one for all."

113

"Technically, that's a saying from the musketeers, not from knights." Harry said.

114

DREAMLAND

Harry unpacked his backpack in his bedroom. His room was simple and neutral with a twin bed and a chest of drawers. He slipped into his pajamas and brushed his teeth in the adjoining bathroom. Freedom! "A john all my own! I can leave the toilet seat up!" When he smiled into the mirror to make sure his mouth was clean, a voice from the mirror shot back with a "Lookin' good!"

"Oh, I love it here!" he said.

"And I love you!" said the mirror.

Harry laughed. "This is wild."

Honey settled into her room. It was exactly what she always imagined her room would be if she was in total control. All she did was think and she had a pretty bed with a white lacy canopy. She thought things like princess lamps with pink shades into existence. It was the most spectacular thing she had ever imagined and it was all true, it was all real.

She sat on her bed and tapped her phone. Facetime. Up until now that was the most amazing marvel of technology in Honey's life. She had planned to talk with Brianna, Becky and Claire tonight. They had gathered in Becky's bedroom which was not nearly as cool as Honey's smart room. But she didn't tell them that.

"Girls, you are not going to believe this!" Honey said. "But this place is spectacular. The house can read my mind. All I have do is think and whatever I'm thinking about happens."

"No way," Claire said. "That's impossible."

"No, it's true. Like right now. I've been thinking about changing my hair."

Honey closed her eyes and thought about hairstyles.

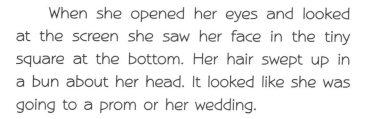

When she opened her eyes and looked at the screen she saw her face in the tiny square at the bottom. Her hair swept up in a bun about her head. It looked like she was going to a prom or her wedding.

"Too much!" screamed Brianna. "Tone it down. Way down."

"Okay," Honey said. Her hair turned as red as Pippi Longstocking's hair, her childhood heroine and then it braided itself into two pigtails as she watched.

The girls howled. "Oh, Pippi! How we miss you!" Becky said.

Honey closed her eyes again. This time her hair turned wavy and sleek. She could have been a movie star.

✐

Harry made his way to the kitchen for a glass of water. On the way he heard the giggling coming from Honey's room. "Girls," he said.

He walked into the kitchen and said, "I'd like a glass of water." And there on the ultra white counter was a glass of water. He sipped it. It was room temperature. Just the way he liked it.

"Wow! This water tastes awesome!" Harry said.

"It comes from Berg in the Swiss Alps. Berg is the town where Mister Modbot was raised. He had it specially brought in for the weekend. By the way, Harry, I know you like to sneak around at night....investigate..."

"How did you know that, COS?"

"I am already learning your likes and habits. But if you would enjoy it, I can deliver the water right to your room. Room temperature, just the way you like it."

"Hey COS, tell me. Do you and Siri hang out much?"

"Oh, that was low, Harry," COS said. Harry could hear the smile in his voice.

"COS, you are amazing!" Harry shook his head. Even Samson Dupree couldn't do the things COS could do.

120

Harry went back to his room. It was late now and he was sleepy. He quickly said his prayers. For Harry, prayers were sometimes more than words. They were his soul projecting into imagined eternity. Then, he hopped into bed. He put his head against the pillow.

"You seem unsure, Harry, of what you'd like to do now," said COS in a soft whisper. "Would you like to read, or watch a movie, or play a video game before you nod off?"

"Thank you, COS," Harry said. "I'll just say goodnight."

"Good night, Harry Moon."

Harry fell right to sleep. While he slept, the Central Operating System read Harry's REM as he dreamed.

✄

Mary and John Moon watched an old movie, *It's a Wonderful Life* with a bucket of freshly popped popcorn in the master bedroom. The movie was not flat against one wall but played around the whole room. The holographic technology was extremely advanced. When Jimmy Stewart and Donna Reed danced in their old high school gymnasium, it seemed like they were dancing across the bed.

"It is truly astounding," said John. "The Modbot Theme Parks were always at the cutting edge of tech. It makes sense that Marvel would be the pathfinder of the smart house."

✄

Harry did not dream that night, or at least, not that he could remember. But in the morning he was greeted by a friendly character he had

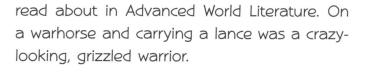

read about in Advanced World Literature. On a warhorse and carrying a lance was a crazy-looking, grizzled warrior.

"There you are Pancho!" said the hologram.

"Pancho?" asked Harry as he wiped the sleep from his eyes.

"I have been looking all over for you, Pancho! Come along! Time to wake! Time to do! We have dragons to slay!"

Harry jumped out of bed. COS had created a friendly persona as a wake-up call from the mind scan. Harry had been reading the massive book, *The Adventures of Don Quixote*, in Miss Pryor's class.

"Shall we chase windmills?" said Don Quixote.

"Let's chase dragons, instead!" said Harry, laughing.

"Very well, dear boy, and upon my horse

we can talk of my favorite subject. Chivalry!"

Harry watched the room become 16th century Spain with a winding country road where Don Quixote rode into the horizon. Harry went running with Don Quixote through his room. Soon enough, Harry was getting quite the morning workout while he and his side kick battled dragons.

☙❧

Wanting to enjoy all that ModPod had to offer, Mary had been up at dawn. She charged into the kitchen in her nightgown and robe.

"Well, good morning, Mary!" said the chef who looked very much like the kindly Julia Child. She was tall and jolly, with a bright blue apron around her waist. She seemed to drift through the kitchen like a ghost. The lovely, white kitchen smelled like an inviting coffee shop.

"Oh! What aroma! Is that Peruvian?" asked Mary.

"You know it, Mary. Your favorite from a little coffee shop on Beacon Street when you were going to nursing school. Do you remember those days, Mary?" asked the hologram.

"Do I!" Mary said. "They were great days."

"They must have been," the chef said.

"Are you Julia Child?" Mary asked. "I love Julia!"

124

"Almost, Mary. I am Wilma Waldorf. Modbot couldn't get Julia's likeness rights, but I can make a heavenly Eggs Benedict as well as Julia. My dear, would you like some freshly brewed Beacon Place Coffee?"

"Why, that sounds lovely, Wilma," said Mary.

A panel opened. A yellow coffee pot hovered in the space. There was also a matching cup and saucer.

"What kind of technology are you, Wilma?" Mary asked as she took a seat at the table. Wilma placed the cup and saucer at Mary Moon's seat and poured.

"Thank you for asking, Mary. I am a force-field hologram. The Modbot Company has yet to be able to perfect an acceptable human droid, so difficult to duplicate the dexterity of the human being and such. All the holograms or holos at the Super ModPod are stand-ins until the droid-tech is perfected. Go ahead and poke at me."

Mary smiled. "Alright then."

She poked Wilma's apron. Her finger passed right through as though Wilma were mist.

"When it looks like I am carrying or pushing or exerting strength, it is a force-field built into my movement. It's all about magnetic energies. Hopefully you forget all that and you will know me as the happy chef here to lend you a hand in your busy day."

"Sounds good." Mary sipped her coffee. "This is great."

"Thank you," Wilma said. "I know you like to spend some time alone and with your reading before you start your day."

As Mary took a sip of coffee, she looked around the kitchen and observed to her delight that it's seamless screens had transformed the room into a pretty flower garden with morning light. Birds sang in the air as she continued to read. She looked up to the ceiling and thought about the sacred words she had stenciled in her own kitchen. The Moon Family Operating System, she called it to her kids. And then the words appeared on the walls – love, peace, kindness – just as they were in her own kitchen on Nightingale Lane.

"I could get use to this," Mary said.

While Mary was enjoying her quiet morning, John Moon was already in the garage.

"Man," he said with a sigh. "I feel like tinkering on my MG-F."

"We can do better than that," COS said.

"How's that, COS?" asked John.

"Why don't we build one with the ModPod 3D Printer?"

"We can do that?" asked John.

"If you can dream it, we can build it," replied COS.

127

EVIL ON WITCH BROOM ROAD

As John looked across the empty garage, a panel opened and standing there was Roger Wrench, the host of John's favorite YouTube video, *This Old Car.*

"Is that you, Roger?" asked John.

"I'm a hologram, John. Together, you and I are going to build a car."

"This weekend?" asked John, incredulously.

"With DeeDeeDee, the 3D Printer. We'll have it built this morning."

"What!" John could hardly believe his ears.

"How else are you going to get to Windermere Dairy today? They're closing the ice cream stand for the season this weekend. Last call, John."

With that, a panel spanning the entire north wall of the garage lifted, exposing a massive lode of steel and glass which seemed to stretch into eternity. For John, the whole garage was humming with excitement.

"What is that?" John asked.

"I'm DeeDeeDee, the 3D printer. I know a guy. His name is COS."

"Let's get to work, boys!" John said.

Honey woke to a strange sound, like water lapping against a boat. She opened her eyes and discovered that her bed had been transformed into a large, flat boat. All around her was the sparkling Nile River projected from the floor-to-ceiling screens. Above her on the ceiling, a crown of green palm fronds blew about under a gentle breeze in the summer blue sky.

131

"Good morning, my queen," said a golden falcon perched in a palm tree. Rising from the bed and stretching, Honey looked into the screen. There she was! But in the screen, she was dressed in a sunny, silk tunic. Golden bangles shone on her arms.

"Oh my gosh! I'm Cleopatra!" she said to the screen.

"That was my favorite Halloween costume of yours!" said the falcon.

"Mine, too!" Honey replied, delighted.

"I thought the old red wagon turned into a chariot was a nice touch," said the falcon.

"We worked hard on that!" Honey said.

"We consulted your mom," the falcon said. "And Wilma Waldorf, the chef, has made your favorite, gluten free pancakes with fat free whipped cream and organic strawberries!"

"Yippee!" Honey cried as she grabbed her robe from the dresser. As she approached the door, it opened for her. Then she remembered. Around her neck was her lovely, heart-shaped, silver amulet from Uncle Marvel.

Honey dashed into the kitchen. Harry was already there, eating his breakfast with Harvest and Mom.

"Good morning, Honey," said the large chef. "You are going to love the warm strawberries on your gluten-free pancakes!"

Honey could hardly wait.

"Where's Dad?" Honey asked.

"He's in the garage working on his car," Harry said.

"His car? He brought the MG-F here?"

"No, he's making a new car," said Harry. "We're going for ice cream later."

133

"All set!" Dad said, as he walked into the kitchen.

"All set for what, Dad?" asked Honey. "Ice cream?"

"All set for a test drive!" Dad said. "Come on, let me introduce you to Hovie."

"Ok, Dad," Honey said. "Just let me finish these pancakes. They are delicious."

"Yeah," Harry said. "And my oatmeal is the best I ever had."

"Okie dokie," Dad said. "Meet me in the garage when you've finished."

When Honey and Harry arrived in the garage, they could hardly believe their eyes. There it was. Hovie. Fire engine red and low to the ground like a race car and wide as a bullet train.

"I've heard of 3D printing, but never imagined it at such large scale," Harry said.

134

"Climb in," Dad said. "It as real as you and me."

Harry sat in Hovie's plush fiber seats.

"I might as well be in *Star Trek*," said Honey as she settled into her seat.

The circle of seats faced inward in a conversational-like design. The inside of Hovie's Pod was sleek and modern with windows from the floor all the way to the apex of the ceiling.

"Put on your seatbelts, gang," Dad said with

a smile. "I'll go get Mom and Harvest."

Soon the whole family joined. Even Buzz and Talia came along for the fun. They all belted up in their comfy and luxurious seats.

"It is so weird to have you not driving," Honey said.

"The future is upon us!" Dad said. "In ten years, everyone will be self-driving."

"Ready, Mr. Moon?" COS asked.

"All set, Hovie!"

As Hovie rose into the air, the north wall, which had once exposed the intricacies of the 3D Printer, now revealed the great outdoors.

"The self drive is all based on game technology," Dad said. "If it hadn't been for the *Sims* and *Minecraft*, we probably wouldn't be riding like this."

Hovie floated out of the garage.

"What do you say we get some ice cream at *Handmade Mountain*?" Dad asked.

"Why not?" said Honey, giggling.

"Sounds like a plan," Harry said with a smile.

"Last weekend before it closes for the winter," Dad said.

"I love their Peanut Butter Mountain Mummy Mashup!" Honey said.

"Shall we make our way to the Mountain?" asked COS.

"You bet," Dad said.

Hovie sailed over Herman Melville Field. It moved on a gravity platform above the road. Dad was enjoying the view. He watched the gorgeous view of the Sleepy Hollow country-side.

"Wow, this is the life!" he said as he leaned back on his chair.

131

"It's true what Marvel Modbot said." Harry said. "At it's best, technology frees us up to enjoy life with the people we care about."

"Wahoo! I feel like Jane Jetson!" Mom said.

"Who's Jane Jetson?" asked Harry.

"Who's Jane Jetson?" said Mary, cheerfully laughing. "Why Jane Jetson is from Orbit City. She's from the future. She's a future mom. Then there's George, her husband, and Judy,

Elroy, and Rosie, the robot maid. Rosie is rather like COS I suppose but with more tin like the Tin Man in Oz. And then, John, I cannot remember - what is the name of their adorable robot dog?"

"Astro!" Dad said.

Honey crossed her arms across her chest and frowned. "Mom, what are you two talking about?"

"The Jetsons. It was a TV series about a family in the future."

"That TV show must have run when dinosaurs ruled the earth," said Honey, as she slouched deeper into her chair.

Hovie arrived at Windermere Dairy Farm where Handmade Haunted Mountain Ice Cream was located. Even the cows in the far field turned their heads as the fire-engine-red spacecraft landed in the gravel parking lot.

The passengers climbed out of the hover-craft. They were greeted by a tall, young man

wearing a blue apron with an image of a mountain eating an ice cream cone on it.

"Hello," he said. "My name is Taylor Windermere the Fourth. Welcome."

"Thank you," Honey said taking the lead. After all, it was her special weekend. She was the star.

"What the heck? Is this part of your weekend?" Taylor asked.

139

"It is, Taylor," Dad said proudly. He draped his arm around Honey. "We are all very proud of Honey."

"I cannot wait for the future," said Taylor. "Man, what a beautiful machine."

After filling up on their favorite ice cream treats, the Moons climbed back into the Hovie. They all settled into their comfy seats. Honey let go a deep, satisfying sigh. "I don't get it," she said.

THE SCARY SMART HOUSE

"What?" Harry asked.

"Why Mayor Kligore doesn't like the Mod Pod."

"How do you know that?" Harry asked.

"I overheard them outside the Haunted Wood Brasserie. The mayor was threatening Uncle Marvel. He said there could only be 'one brand' in Sleepy Hollow, and only 'one house, for a house divided will not stand'."

140

Harry leaned back in his seat and the Hovie took off. He looked out the window at the passing sights. As he watched the road, Harry saw the black Lustro Phantom with the We Drive By Night license plates passing in the opposite direction. He shuddered.

⌒⌒

"Will you get a gander of that disgusting Modbot thing, Boss Man! said Cherry Tomato. She was driving the black Phantom. Mayor Maximus Kligore sat next to her. Shotgun. "Is it

even legal?"

"Yet another violation," Kligore said.

Cherry yanked the radio mike from the dash board and roared into its speaker, "Calling Officer Ortiz, Calling Officer..."

The mayor pulled the radio mike away from Cherry Tomato's mouth. "Good thinking but, as you know, girl, we have bigger steaks to grill."

141

"Ok, ok, sorry Boss."

"Miss Tomato, do you understand the elemental aspects of power?"

"Hit me up, Boss Man," she said.

"Links. It has everything to do with links. You are new to magic. I am adept. The more you can link to every aspect of power, the stronger your magic. I pull from the power of the ebbing tides. I link it with the energy that wafts from violence and from war. I link it with

the fear of the dark and the fright rising from not knowing."

"Oh wowzers," Cherry said. "That sounds dangerous." She smacked her gum.

"Guess what, Miss Tomato?" Kligore said.

"What Boss Man?"

"Tonight, when I hack into Modbot's operating system, the power that is linked to mine will include the energy of the fallen angels."

Cherry gripped the wheel as tight as she can. "Ooooo, Boss Man. That sounds exciting."

142

DON'T BE AFRAID
OF THE DARK

The Hovie settled into the garage as easily as slipping on a glove.

"That was awesome," Harry said. "This is the best weekend ever!"

"It sure is. And you owe it all to me," Honey glowed.

"No, now," Mom said. "No bragging. It's been a long and exciting day. Let's just get settled for the night."

Harry and Honey dashed to the ModPod front portal. It didn't take long for the change into PJs and request a salty snack from COS. Mom and Dad put Harvest down for the night.

144

"Now, you guys have fun," Dad said.

"But not too much fun," Mom said with a wink.

Harry had just found an interesting TV show to watch, a magic show starring his idol, world renowned magician Elvis Gold, when he heard a strange noise.

"Did you hear that?" he asked Honey who had her nose buried in book.

"Yeah," Honey said. "It sounded like the front

moment please."

The door opened.

"Come on in, Mrs. Middlemarch," said Honey. "Welcome to the ModPod."

Mildred hurried right in.

"Follow us," Harry said. "You won't believe this place."

146

Mrs. Middlemarch sat down in a plush white

door. If this place has a front door."

"Come on," Harry said. "Let's check it out."

"Are you sure?" Honey asked. "That's a little creepy."

"Awww, Buzz will protect us," Harry said.

But before they could get to the door they heard voices. And one of them was COS.

145

"Good evening, Mildred," COS. "How can I help you?"

"You know my name?" Mrs. Middlemarch asked.

"Hey. That's Mrs. Middlemarch," Harry said.

"What's she doing here? Maybe she wants to do another interview with the world's greatest essayist." Honey beamed at Harry.

"Why, yes, you were at the reception when we arrived the other day," COS answered. "One

chair. A soft voice emanated from the room.

"Here's some hot sassafras tea with lemon, Mildred," said COS. "Just the way you like it."

Mrs. Middlemarch gasped. "What the heck! How did it know that is my favorite tea?"

Honey laughed. "That's just COS."

On the white table, a portal opened from the surface and a cup of steaming tea appeared.

147

"Isn't it cool?" Honey said. "COS has gotten to know us and filled the house with all the stuff we love."

Mrs. Middlemarch looked all around. "Oh dear," she said, pointing to one of the screens. "That's you, Honey, dressed as the legendary warrior Princess Reanna with her army of good faeries. And Brianna, Claire, and Becky in their diaphanous dresses."

"And that's me," Harry said. He pointed

to himself dressed as a knight fighting both a dragon and a windmill with an old, heroic Don Quixote.

"And that's just Dad," Honey said. "He's supposed to be at NASCAR with Hovie. But he's so lame."

"Doesn't this all seem a little strange?" said Mrs. Middlemarch.

148

"Are you kidding, Mrs. Middlemarch? This has been a total blast!" said Harry.

"No, I mean that I am here?" she said.

"Yes, why are you here Mrs. Middlemarch?" Honey asked. "To do another story?"

She sipped her tea. Honey couldn't help but notice that Mrs. Middlemarch's hand was shaking.

"My car stopped for no reason on Witch Broom Road. There's a full tank of gas and I had it in the shop just a month ago. I tried to call Ichabod's Garage. My cell phone has been off all day. It's Family Unplug Saturday at our house, so my cell was never used. I had no power. The battery was totally dead. Doesn't it all seem strange?"

Honey took a deep breath. "Not if you happen to be Editor and Chief of the town newspaper and your boss is looking for some bad publicity."

"Mildred! What a surprise!" Dad said. "What brings you here?"

Before Mrs. Middlemarch could answer, the power went off.

The house went black. Everyone gasped. Honey Moon clutched her neck for the silver amulet.

It was gone.

"My amulet," she cried. "It's gone. Where did it go? I haven't taken it off at all. Not even once."

"Don't worry," Dad said. "we'll find it. Right now, the house is on the fritz. COS will fix it."

"Come on," Harry said. "To COS."

They moved as quickly as they could down the corridor to COS's headquarters.

COS whirled and spun in the small pod at the end of the corridor. His friendly countenance had disappeared, morphed into ugly anger. The friendly man in the moon face was gone. Instead, Honey shrieked at the sight of an evil jack o' lantern with craggy teeth, small eyes, and a leering open smile staring out from the face of the orb. There was a flicker of light over the silver ball. Then the pod flickered as dark as the house.

Honey heard crying.

"It's Harvest!" she said. "Where's Mom? I'm really frightened. Daddy?"

Honey took her Dad's hand. "We have to go get Harvest."

150

"Harvest," called Harry as he got down on his knees and fumbled in the dark to the entranceway of the living room.

"Harry! I'm scared!" Harvest said.

"Don't worry, I'm coming to get you, little buddy."

"He's afraid of the dark," Honey said.

"I know, sweet pea," said Mom.

161

"I know. I know. I'm coming to get you!" Harry said as he crawled across the carpet. As he reached into the murk, Harry felt the little arm of the toddler. He grabbed hold of his baby brother who started sobbing.

"Oh my stars!" said Mrs. Middlemarch. "This is so frightening."

"Everyone remain calm," said Talia Fetching, as she stumbled through the dark into the room.

"This is impossible," said Buzz Goodmorrow. "The power seems to have been cut and the fire door will not open. Who would do this? Honey, are you in here?"

"I am here, Buzz," came Honey's voice from the dark.

"Can you signal the amulet?"

"It's gone," Honey said. "I noticed it was gone when the lights went out."

"What? Are you sure?"

"Yes," she said.

"Can you get to the amulet?" Talia asked in the darkness of the great room.

"I don't know where it is," Honey said.

"Where did you see it last?" Talia asked.

"Not to freak anyone out, but after the girls left the Princess Reanna party this afternoon, came by and we went over to her house. I forgot all about the cobra but I think that maybe it snatched the amulet."

"Was it a red cobra?" Harry asked.

"It was. How did you know?" Honey asked.

"The mayor has Oink and Oink has Ug. But Maximus's boss, B L Zebub has got a red cobra."

154

"What's his name?" asked Honey.

"We're not on a first name basis," said Harry. "But I don't have to know it to say that cobra is evil."

Harry didn't understand how it was even possible, but the dark grew even darker. Harry felt the blackness pervading him. Harry whispered, "ABRACADABRA," hoping to bring light into the dark. But whatever curse was upon the smart house had negated his magic, too. It must have been extremely powerful, because as he called out to Rabbit, Rabbit did not answer. Harry

I returned to my barge on the Nile. It was lovely, but then something freaky happened in the middle of the virtual reality."

"What happened?" Dad asked.

"There was a pretty woven basket next to me. I opened it and inside there was a cobra. I was scared so I went to close the lid but the lid was gone! The cobra said that it wouldn't bite if I just charmed it."

Honey wanted to cry but she stopped herself. Be brave, she said to herself. Be Brave.

"So I picked up the little wooden flute and started to play. Well, the cobra began to rise. It seemed very happy, bobbing its head in joy. Then, just like that, it leaped up, not to strike me, but to thank me for my song." Honey sucked in a deep breath. She didn't like it that she couldn't see anyone.

"The cobra was on me. I threw it off the barge. I have a feeling that was not part of the software program. Then Pippi Longstocking felt panic grow in his spirit. This had never happened before. In this desperate moment as the power of destruction flooded him, Harry Moon began to believe that maybe there was no Rabbit at all.

"Let's try the entrance and exit portals," said Buzz Goodmorrow.

"I'll help," said Mrs. Middlemarch.

"Let's go," Dad said.

165

"You take Harvest," said Mom as she lurched forward with the toddler and managed to get him into Harry's arms. "And stay put!" she said as her voice trailed off. Harry was fine with staying put. Where would he go? He did not have Samson's impenetrable magic cape. He did not have Rabbit. As hard as he tried to wiggle the fingers of his power hand through the window of eternity, he could not find a way to access his magic.

"Harry?"

"Is that you, Honey?" Harry said.

"Yes. Give me your hand."

"No," said Harry. "I have Harvest."

But then Harvest slipped out of Harry's arms and onto the floor. Harry felt his little brother hug his right leg as if he was holding on for dear life. ""Don't let go, pal," Harry said.

"If you are my friend, you'll give me your hand," said Honey. Harry flinched as her fingers poked his ribcage.

"I'm not your friend. I am your brother," said Harry, backing away. He wanted to focus on the funk and desperation flooding through him.

"And I'm your sister. That's not what I am talking about," said Honey. "Haven't we learned something important on this amazing adventure? That we can be more than brother and sister. We can actually like each other."

"And I'm not liking you much right now,"

Harry said, standing as rigid as he could while Harvest pulled on his leg. "You should have come to me about that red cobra in the charm basket."

"At the time I didn't think much of it," she said. "How about this? How about you like me because you love me?"

"Liking is harder than loving you."

"You know a house divided will not stand, Harry," said Honey. "And the bad guys may want to bring this house down, but they will never break our family up."

"If we survive at all," Harry said.

"We will if you will take my hand and call me 'friend'," said Honey.

"Okay, Okay," he said, grabbing for her hand in the dark.

"Be nice," Honey said softly.

"Okay, nice.... friend," said Harry as he grabbed her hand.

As he did, he could see her face in the dark. She smiled softly and wonderfully. Her eyes opened to him and Harry swallowed hard. He thought he was going to cry. But then as he looked, the light moved off her face.

"Hey Rabbit!" cried Harvest, reminding Harry that his little brother was the only one besides Harry that could see the harlequin.

"What?" said Harry as he watched the glow of Rabbit shine through his sister.

Harvest reached up and took Rabbit's paw and pulled him, making Rabbit and Honey two. The light from Rabbit shone on the two brothers and their sister.

"The evil principality had engulfed you," Rabbit said. "I could not reach you, Harry. So I turned to a friend. Don't be afraid of the dark, Harry. Don't be afraid of the dark, Honey, or you Harvest," said Rabbit as he held Harvest's hand and looked to Honey and Harry. "For too long, we have believed we should be afraid of the dark. But the darkness is where most life begins. The seed opens in the dark soil. The chickling breaks through the dark wall of the egg. The skull protects our minds in total darkness so that our thoughts might sparkle with light. It is the dark womb which brings the world it's many children. It was the Great Magician's light that traveled over the dark waters in the beginning. He promised us we will always have a moon and stars to guide us through the night, and if you cannot find that light, then look for his shining magic.

159

"Don't be afraid of the dark, my friends. Evil can live anywhere. It travels through the dark as well as the sunshine. So be watchful for evil, yet don't fear it. Life chose you, all of you, as all worldlings are chosen, to be the light against evil – against the selfish, the un-caring, the brutal, the violent and the destruc-tive. There will always be trouble, my friends, so there will always be a time for heroes. And there isn't a hero on this earth who doesn't need a friend."

"Can I reach through the window and touch eternity?" Harry asked Rabbit.

"Try," said Rabbit.

"Abracadabra," Harry incanted. He opened his fingers and he could feel the magic return to his palms. Harry smiled at Rabbit.

Harry raised his hands, his palms flat, parallel to the floor. As they ascended, the room grew bright with light.

"Thanks Rabbit," said Harry.

"Don't thank me, thank your friend. She opened the path for me to reach you," Rabbit said. Harry felt like a kid on Christmas morning. He turned around and hugged Honey.

"Alright, alright, that's a little too much like," said Honey. "Kinda icky."

"Remember," Rabbit said. "A red cobra is still just a cobra even if he does work for the Chairman of *We Drive By Night*. Don't let any cobra have power over you, whether blue or red." Then Rabbit was gone to the three of them.

"Snack time!" shouted Wilma Waldorf from the kitchen, the power restored.

"Whew!" said Honey. "Back to normal!"

"Not quite!" shouted Wilma. "Come on, kids, get your midnight snack!" Then, they heard the whoosh of a fork against a carving knife.

161

162

HORRIBLE HOVIE

It was dark in the garage until John Moon could get to the Hovie. Once he opened the door, he discovered Hovie had its own power source, separate from the car. The interior light for the fire engine red Hovie lit up. The light panel was soft and dim but it was still light.

"Bingo!" John cried. Talia, Buzz, and Mary

stood outside the vehicle while Mary clapped her hands in excitement.

"I'll go grab the kids!" Mary said.

"Not so fast!" said the voice of Hovie.

"You don't sound like COS," said John as he moved out of the swivel chair toward the door.

"COS is on bathroom break. There's a new driver in town," the voice said. A rush of energy, rattling like a train leaving the station, surged from the car. Talia was thrown into the air. She sailed through the dark garage, her legs flailing until she was pulled through the door. Buzz was the second one to be sucked into Hovie. Mary Moon turned and ran towards the door. As she ran, the 3D printer, DeeDeeDee roared, opened its wall and spit out a fully-formed Modbot Theme Park employee.

"You're not going anywhere, mom," said the Modbot, pushing Mary into the vehicle. "Step right this way. Enjoy the ride." His eyes were green and his teeth were black with rot.

"My kids!" Mary cried.

"Your kids are in our capable hands," sneered the green-eyed modbot. He shoved Mary into Hovie. "In fact, they're getting a little midnight snack as we speak."

Buzz sat in the swivel chair. " I don't understand," he said. "How could a bug get into the operating system?"

"A bug?" said the voice of Hovie with sharp disdain. "I would hardly call myself a bug."

Hovie's windows lit up with bright light. The red Cobra was in each window panel like a program lighting up the banks of screens at Best Buy. "Call me Red Cobra!" The cobra's scaly head was draped in rusty scales. His eyes were as green as the Modbot employee. He opened his mouth and a cloven tongue flicked out from the screen.

"You're nothing more than a security breech," said Buzz with a smirk.

"No, I am the magic that owns this town." The snaked hissed. "Time to go. Fasten those seat belts tight!"

With a lurch, Hovie rose off the floor. Hovie shot out of the garage and onto Herman Melville Field.

"It seems to have a life of its own," said John.

With furrowed panic in her brow, Talia Fetching unstrapped herself from her chair and walked to the front of Hovie. There were no Star Trek

controls, no fancy pulsing lights. Hovie, like all of Super ModPod elements, remained, or so it seemed, voice activated.

"R92," Talia said, directing her voice at the grey, empty dashboard. "R92," Talia repeated, her voice growing in volume.

"What are you doing, Talia?" asked John as Hovie bucked up and down on Witch Broom Road.

"It's the numerical code for a reboot. Talia's trying to override the Central Operating System," answered Buzz.

"Try. Try. Try," said Red Cobra. "So sad. I told you. There's a new driver in town."

168

MIDNIGHT SNACK

Harry, Honey, and Harvest headed into the kitchen. Harry bumped into Mrs. Middlemarch, wandering about the pod.

"Oh, Harry!" she said, startled. "It's you!" She pulled him in for a hug. "Is this the tour?"

"No, Mrs. Middlemarch. There is no tour. Do you know where my parents are and Buzz and Talia?" asked Honey.

"I think they may still be on the tour," Mrs. Middlemarch said.

Wilma Waldorf, the hologram, stood there with her big apron. The room seemed rather eerie. There was a fiery candelabra in the center of the table with silver serving domes at each seat. Wilma Waldorf did not seem herself. Her silver hair was standing straight out. The whites of her eyes were cracked. Spidery blood vessels ran through the cracks.

"Mrs. Waldorf, do you know where my parents are?" asked Harry.

"They're around here somewhere," she said.

"Cheerios?" asked Harvest.

"I have hot food for you tonight! You'll eat what I serve you!"

Mrs. Middlemarch shouted, "Give the kid his Cheerios!"

Wilma Waldorf laughed and opened a portal from the ceiling. Cheerios rained down on Harvest's head. Harvest looked down at the cereal on the floor and cried.

171

"Uh oh," said Honey as she pointed to the sacred words that had previously encircled the ceiling. "Looks like the new operating system

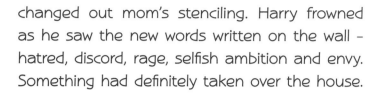

changed out mom's stenciling. Harry frowned as he saw the new words written on the wall – hatred, discord, rage, selfish ambition and envy. Something had definitely taken over the house.

Harry swallowed. His heart pounded.

"Come along, now, don't dawdle and sit down," Wilma Waldorf said. "Those missing people will be with us shortly". The kids and Mrs. Middlemarch sat down at the table. Wilma lifted the silver dome of one of the plates. There was a small roasted hen with Buzz Goodmorrow's head on it.

"Eat me!" said Buzz's tiny head. It was no larger than an apple.

Honey screamed. Harvest gasped. Harry sized up the situation while Mrs. Middlemarch recorded on her phone.

"No, don't scream," shouted Wilma Waldorf. "There's plenty for everyone!" Racing around the table, Wilma pulled the silver domes from the white china plates.

"Eat me!" cried Dad's head, small as a tomato, high on a plate of steaming macaroni.

"Eat me!" shouted the head of Talia Fetching. Her head was on the neck of a roasted pheasant.

Wilma Waldorf lifted another dome to reveal Mom's head. Her head was on a meatball, atop a hill of marinara sauce and spaghetti.

173

Harry shouted as he got up. "Come on, it's not real! They're holograms!"

"This house has gone insane!" Honey said. "Stark, raving mad."

"It's sure going to make a heck of a story for *Awake!*" Mrs. Middlemarch cried. "That is, if we can get out of here alive."

"They don't want to kill us," cried Honey. "They just want to make sure that Smart Town never happens!"

The gang ran out of the kitchen.

"Wow, such spit and fire," Harry said. "Princess Reanna has really rubbed off on you!" said Harry.

"Princess Reanna isn't real either! But I am and you are, Harry Moon, and we are Nightingale Knights!"

"Where are we going?" asked Mrs. Middlemarch.

"The Nightingale Knights are taking back their castle!" "But how?" she said as they ran down the corridor.

"We're going to install OUR operating system," called Harry. He held out his power hand and threw the white panel from the door at the end of the hall.

"Follow me!" Harry shouted. He really did not have to shout. Honey and Mrs. Middlemarch were on him like glue.

Harry entered the room of blue light where COS turned. Atop the shining silver globe, Red Cobra was coiled.

"Come in, Harry Moon. I have been waiting a long time for this," hissed the cobra.

Honey and Mrs. Middlemarch stormed the room.

"We've come to reboot," said Honey.

"I don't need new boots. In fact, I don't need boots at all," Red Cobra said as he slapped his tail against the surface of the orb.

"We want Honey's amulet back!" said Harry.

"Why?" hissed the cobra. "Don't you think I wear it well?" He slapped his tail against the orb again. He arched his body to show off Honey's heart-shaped amulet.

"Because we know what you are, you evil thing!" said Honey. "You are cold.

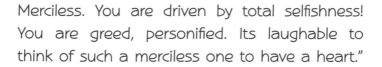

Merciless. You are driven by total selfishness! You are greed, personified. Its laughable to think of such a merciless one to have a heart."

"My, my. You are the one with the words," said the cobra. "Meanwhile, I have your parents and the others orbiting above us and I am about to bring them crashing down on this silly smart house."

"No you will not!" said Harry. "You are but a curse on a system and I will unravel you by the mighty words."

"By the way, that reminds me, Harry, where is your furry friend?" asked the cobra.

"Rabbit is here!" Harry said, marching forward toward the orb. "He is here with me always!"

"I am so scared!" the cobra said.

The cobra arched his back into the air. He was face-to-face with Harry.

"Do you really think your Abracadabra nonsense is going to work against the Chairman of the Board's Chief of Staff?" asked Red Cobra.

"Our operating system will," said Honey Moon. She was in the same place as when she extended her hand to Harry in the darkness. She was emboldened by the presence of Rabbit. Now it was Harry who took her hand.

"Skin for skin, cobra," said Harry. "We are going to shed you and shred you."

"And you know what, snake?" said Honey. "We will use Harry's good magic. Why debase our words in front of you?"

"Maybe because I rule the world?" said Red Cobra. His green eyes shone in the dim blue light of the room.

"You may rule it," said Harry, "but it's not yours. I'm coming to take it back."

"We'll see about that. Ready for Hovie to come crashing down on your heads?"

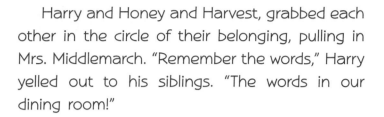

Harry and Honey and Harvest, grabbed each other in the circle of their belonging, pulling in Mrs. Middlemarch. "Remember the words," Harry yelled out to his siblings. "The words in our dining room!"

It was true that Rabbit could not be seen, but he was running through Harry, Honey, and Harvest like an electrical charge.

There may have been those in the neighborhood and in Sleepy Hollow who laughed at the Moons.

But it was true. The Moon family were Nightingale Knights.

◦◊◦

Hovie stopped its roller coaster tilts over the ModPod smart house. Hovie slowed. It began to drift.

"What is this?" said Talia Fetching, her face pale.

"Huh?" said Buzz Goodmorrow. He looked out the window as Hovie did what it was named for. It hovered.

Like a feather held by a gentle wind, Hovie descended from the star-drenched sky.

In the dim blue light of the room of the Central Operating System, the Moon children and Mrs. Middlemarch watched as Red Snake evaporated from the silver globe. The only thing left atop the orb was Honey's heart-shaped silver amulet.

179

"That's the message, isn't it?" Honey asked. "The good heart trumps greed."

"Heroes are never about greed," Harry confirmed.

Hovie had reached the ground and land-ed near the smart house. As Hovie stopped moving, a bell rang.

"What was that, Buzz?" asked John Moon.

"Reboot," answered Buzz.

Mary hugged John.

"Welcome, Moon Family," COS said. "May you enjoy your super ModPod Dream Experience!"

"Oh Harry, I am better than real," replied Rabbit, "I am true."

THE MORNING NEWS

In any small town, news travels fast. It traveled especially fast that Sunday afternoon in Sleepy Hollow when the futuristic helicopter owned by Marvel Modbot flew across the town square, past the Headless Horseman Statue and landed in Herman Melville Field. Buzz Goodmorrow and Talia Fetching had managed to reach

Marvel about the corrupted operating system. Marvel was relieved that everyone in the Moon family was alright after the attack of the runaway COS. He hugged Honey and Harry and thanked their parents for being so understanding.

"I am so sorry," he said to Honey. The tycoon was standing in the rubble of what had once been the dream kitchen with Honey and Harry.

"But it was not your fault, Mr. Modbot. It was evil. Evil is insidious. It can ruin even the best dream weekend. The point is, you tried to do something good."

"I guess we remain in beta testing until we can add additional fail safes against the evil principalities," he said. "We have our work cut out for us."

"We will always have work to do," Harry said as he remembered what Rabbit had told him in the dark. "As beautiful as our world is, there will always be trouble in it, so we will always

have the chance to be heroes."

Marvel Modbot patted Harry on the shoulder.

"I like your spirit, Harry!" said Marvel.

"It's the spirit we all share," added Honey.

"I call it my gut," said Marvel as he grabbed his belly which had probably seen too much Treasure Hunt Surprise over the years. Then he stuck his pointer finger to the ceiling, signaling the world beyond. "But I know where my gut comes from."

183

"What will you do about Monday's Town Meeting?" asked Harry.

"I'm going to ask the town to hold off the decision for Smart Town until we can perfect our system. We will come back when ModPod Incorporated is truly ready to talk and that I guarantee. The battle may be over. But the war is not."

"That makes sense," said Honey. "That way you admit further progress is needed, and take away the sting of failure." Harry was impressed with his sister. While he was perfecting his skills in magic, she was sharpening her mind.

"I will tell you one thing, Harry and Honey. It is what my gut told me," Marvel said, grabbing his belly again. "It told me not to trust the *We Drive By Night S Corp* or its chairman."

184

"Your gut can join the club with my turtle and Harry's rabbit," said Honey.

The news had traveled everywhere before Mildred Middlemarch's banner headline ran on Monday morning about the dangers of the Super ModPod. There were plenty of incriminating pictures in the Monday paper, and a gallery of one hundred and thirty-five pictures and twenty two videos on the *Awake in Sleepy Hollow* website. But Marvel Modbot was a true pro. As he had promised the Moons, Marvel went before Town Meeting and asked that a vote not be conducted until they had perfected the system. He publicly apologized to Honey and the Moon Family and thanked them for their understanding.

Outside the town hall where the meeting took place, Honey and Harry walked over to Marvel Modbot amidst the crowd of townspeople. They had come to say goodbye.

"Not so fast," Marvel said. "Before we really say goodbye," he said with mischief in his voice, "I think someone might need a taste of some Treasure Hunt Surprise!"

185

The Tuesday headline *Awake in Sleepy Hollow* could not have been clearer if anyone had not heard the news. *Spooky Town Sends Smart Town Running!* There, on the front page of the paper was Marvel Modbot, the chairman of one of the most successful companies in the world, waving goodbye to the people of Sleepy Hollow. He and his endeavor clearly looked like a failure. Mildred Middlemarch felt badly about the positioning of the story but Maximus Kligore had pressured her, and while the paper was printed with disappearing ink, that headline was around for a few more days.

Miss Cherry Tomato could certainly read that simple newspaper banner. She giggled with delight. Her merry way was infectious. As Mayor Maximus Kligore entered the outer office with his morning coffee, he was caught up in the cheerful festivities. Normally stoic, the mayor could not have been more overjoyed with the direction Town Meeting had taken and the way Tuesday's headline read. He took Cherry Tomato's hands and together they danced a fast tango.

"Boss Man, you are the best!" she sang, clicking her fingers as if they were castanets.

As he entered his office, Maximus Kligore tossed the paper onto his desk and placed his hot coffee on a coaster. He pulled his elegant red leather chair away from the desk to sit. He shrieked so loud that even Cherry Tomato heard it in the next room.

Coiled contentedly atop the red leather chair was Red Cobra.

"Get out of my chair!" shouted Maximus Kligore. Red Cobra's eyes darted upward like a cobra in a charm basket.

187

Maximus screamed so loud that he couldn't hear the laughter at the windowsill.

"Get out, I said!" Maximus shouted once more. This time he pointed to the door. "Or I will throw you out!"

The cobra struck. In moments, the cobra wrapped himself around Maximus Kligore's body. That cobra grew as tall and thick as the mayor.

188

"You fool! The curse is not on me!" he screamed. Cherry Tomato ran into the office and hurled herself at the giant cobra. She beat on the monster with both fists.

"Unhand Boss Man!" she shouted.

But her fists were going right through the cobra's body onto the shoulders of Kligore. And when Kligore held up his hands, they were in defense against Cherry Tomato's manic swings.

The wrestling match continued against the

cobra as Maximus and Cherry crashed through the outer office and through the open door to the town square.

It was only then that Mayor Maximus Kligore realized that it was not Red Cobra at all. It was a hologram, a final parting gift. Marvel Modbot had delivered a special treasure hunt surprise just for the mayor.

Honey and Harry both gave the toy titan high fives as they watched from the side of the town hall building. Then Marvel boarded a helicopter, promising to return when he perfected the operating system against an evil security breech, if indeed, he ever could.

189

190

WINTER

According to the weather report, Sleepy Hollow would get it's first dusting of snow that afternoon. *This morning might be the last time I can ride my bike until spring*, Harry thought. It was Saturday morning, after all. He had no particular place to go. The morning sky was extraordinary. It blushed with a soft sea blue. He put his cell phone on mute.

He scrunched his ear buds into his jeans. He pumped his legs and just went. Maybe he'd go see Hao or Declan. Maybe, he'd just ride. The bare branches of the trees lining Nightingale Lane reached aggressively into the sky. It was as if the trees, having lost their coat of colored leaves, were looking for the new, soft coat of a first snow. "Don't worry, trees," Harry said, "snow will come soon enough."

A carol of cardinals sang from branches on Witch Broom Road. "Honey said the Eureka moment could come any time" thought Harry, "that your feet just had to be moving and you weren't thinking about anything." As he pumped his legs past Windermere Dairy Farm, its ice cream stand closed for the winter, Harry Moon had a magical feeling. Surely, Rabbit was with him, but even Rabbit was not speaking in words. Like the trees, like the clouds, like the faraway mountains, Harry was hearing them all.

In this moment nothing could hurt him. There was no pain. Here, liking was as easy as loving. The great piercing of his heart made him overflow with joy. What was this? Was this Eureka? Nothing came to him but for a quiet sense of goodness. He knew he screwed up here and there but, on the whole, he was doing pretty well. Then he thought about Mrs.

Brewster and what she said the day he dropped off Honey's essay. The soft blue sky was growing iron black. The snow clouds were rolling in.

He smiled as he disappeared down Witch Broom Road. She was right. Harry's great life was here now.

M

195

196

MARK ANDREW POE

The Adventures of Harry Moon author Mark Andrew Poe never thought about being a children's writer growing up. His dream was to love and care for animals, specifically his friends in the rabbit community.

Along the way, Mark became successful in all sorts of interesting careers. He entered the print and publishing world as a young man and his company did really, really well.

Mark became a popular and nationally sought-after health care advocate for the care and well-being of rabbits.

Years ago, Mark came up with the idea of a story about a young man with a special connection to a world of magic, all revealed through a remarkable rabbit friend. Mark worked on his idea for several years before building a collaborative creative team to help bring his idea to life. And Harry Moon was born.

In 2014, Mark began a multi-book print series project intended to launch *The Adventures of Harry Moon* into the youth marketplace as a hero defined by a love for a magic where love and 'DO NO EVIL' live. Today, Mark continues to work on the many stories of Harry Moon. He lives in suburban Chicago with his wife and his 25 rabbits.

BE SURE TO READ THE CONTINUING AND
AMAZING ADVENTURES OF HARRY MOON

Harry Moon  Book Club

Become a member of the
Harry Moon Book Club and receive another
of Harry's adventure every other month along
with a magician's hat full of goodies!

Hop over to **www.harrymoon.com**
and sign up today.

Also In the Harry Moon Library:

Graphic novel